She tried to scream, but nothing came out.

The car was gaining ground, nearly to her. The driver had to see her. She was the only target in the vehicle's lights. And it didn't slow down. In fact, it was gaining speed.

Mandy managed a stumbled step as the car came faster and faster. Without a doubt she was about to die.

Suddenly an arm clamped her around the waist. It scooped her off her feet and sent her sailing out of the path of the car just as it careened by.

Mandy clenched her arms around Luke's shoulders. She had no intention of letting go.

"It's okay. You're all right." Luke's chest rumbled against her side as he spoke into her ear, the even rise and fall of his shoulders resetting the tempo for her own. "It's gone. It didn't hit you."

Her breath caught on a hitch. "Or—or you?"

"I'm fine." His voice didn't even wobble.

How could he possibly be so calm when someone had just tried to run her over?

Someone had tried to kill her.

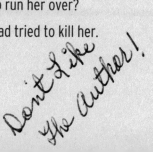

By day **Liz Johnson** is a marketing manager at a Christian publisher. She makes time to write late at night and is a two-time ACFW Carol Award finalist. She lives in Nashville and enjoys exploring local music and theater, and she makes frequent trips to Arizona to dote on her nieces and nephews. She writes stories filled with heart, humor and happily-ever-afters and can be found online at lizjohnsonbooks.com.

Books by Liz Johnson

Love Inspired Suspense

Men of Valor

A Promise to Protect
SEAL Under Siege
Navy SEAL Noel
Navy SEAL Security

Witness Protection

Stolen Memories

The Kidnapping of Kenzie Thorn
Vanishing Act
Code of Justice

Visit the Author Profile page at Harlequin.com.

NAVY SEAL
SECURITY

LIZ JOHNSON

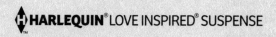

Recycling programs
for this product may
not exist in your area.

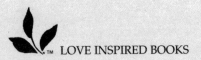

LOVE INSPIRED BOOKS

ISBN-13: 978-0-373-44722-0

Navy SEAL Security

www.Harlequin.com

Printed in U.S.A.

Do not be afraid. Stand firm and you will see
the deliverance the Lord will bring you today.
—Exodus 14:13

For the men and women of the United States military,
both active duty and veteran.
Your sacrifice does not go unnoticed.
Your service is forever appreciated.
May God bless and protect you.

ONE

If Luke Dunham didn't see another white coat until his last day on earth, it would still be too soon.

But he'd made a promise to his senior chief's wife.

He clattered to a stop at the foot of the slanted ramp in front of a nondescript brick building, which looked just like every other in the medical complex. His gaze shifted from the steps at the front of the building to the too-short metal crutches digging into his sides.

Stairs or the ramp?

A low fire burned in his chest, and he squeezed his eyes closed against the flames that licked at his heart.

For years he hadn't cared. Either way was fine. Either got him where he needed to go.

Now he cared.

Now he didn't have an option.

He swung his left leg forward. The white brace succeeded in protecting his knee and also throwing him off-balance. Shoving one of his crutches out to the side, he caught himself just before his foot touched the ground.

He'd already made that mistake once. There was a reason his doctor had told him to stay off it at all costs.

It hurt. Like an inferno.

Like he'd taken another piece of shrapnel along that roadside in Lybania.

He opened his mouth, a pained groan on the tip of his tongue, but he bit it back when the glass door at the top of the ramp flew open. A teenage girl bounced out, her strides so even he barely noticed that one of the knees below her shorts was wrapped in a black brace.

She flipped her long blond hair over her shoulder and shot him a shy smile as she started down the ramp.

He tried to return her gesture, but the IED that had stolen his ability to walk had also made it hard to find genuine happiness. He settled for a shallow dip of his chin and lumbered out of her way.

When the girl was halfway to him, the office door swung open and a woman with orange hair popped out.

"Juliana," she said, before chasing the teen for five short steps.

Juliana's one-eighty was less graceful than her forward motion, requiring at least two extra steps and the aid of the handrail, but her knee remained stable.

The wild-haired woman held out a bag, at which Juliana laughed, high and sweet. "Thanks, Tara." Juliana slipped skinny arms through the straps, sliding a small backpack in place. "See you next week." With that, she executed another awkward turn and ambled past him.

Luke looked up at the woman still leaning against the handrail, her arms now folded over her neon-green scrubs.

Was this Tara the Dr. Berg everyone said was so amazing? The physical therapist his senior chief on the teams, Matt, was convinced had gotten him back in fighting shape after his leg injury? But Matt's injury hadn't been a blown knee. He'd had a couple dozen stitches in his calf, a minor injury to his muscle.

Luke, on the other hand, had shredded every major ligament in his knee.

The doctor at Walter Reed Medical Center had offered him a medical discharge after that first scan. He'd told

Luke there wasn't much hope for a return to active duty. And every doctor thereafter had agreed.

But Luke had promised Ashley Waterstone, the senior chief's wife, that he'd schedule a consultation with Matt's physical therapist.

Squinting into the late-afternoon sun, he shuffled until he'd cut the distance between them in half. "I'm Luke Dunham."

The woman's gaze slid over him like a sculptor searching for imperfections in her masterpiece.

He'd been on the receiving end of that simultaneously curious and knowing stare before. And he'd enjoyed it for a few years. When he was younger. In his early days as a SEAL.

Now it made his stomach churn and his skin feel clammy, even in the warm San Diego air. "I'm early. But I have an appointment with Dr. Berg."

"Of course you do, honey." She gave a sharp nod and walked back to hold the front door open for him. Such a little gesture, but it still set his hands to itching. His dad had taught him that a man held the door open for a woman. Period.

That he couldn't even do it for himself set off that blazing ache in his chest again.

"I'm Tara, Dr. Berg's office manager."

Matt had promised that working with her would change his life.

Maybe.

But that would require a life. And he wasn't sure he had much of one left.

At least this was just a recon mission. He hadn't committed to anything beyond talking with the good doctor... and picking up milk for his mom on the way home.

Tara was still standing with the door wide-open, and Luke hadn't moved an inch. She raised her eyebrows and nodded inside, silently asking what was taking him so long. Sucking in a fortifying breath, he pressed his palms against the rubber grips of his crutches and began a slow lumber up the incline. As he reached the open entrance, a blast of cold air greeted him.

"Is it always a meat locker in here?"

Tara shrugged one shoulder as she led the way across a mostly typical medical waiting room. Sturdy chairs lined three walls, except for three conspicuous holes that could only be there for those who brought their own seats. The usual industrial carpet had been swapped for hardwood, which was easier to maneuver on.

He fell into one of the chairs and poked his tongue in his cheek as he took the clipboard that Tara held out to him.

"Fill that out, and then someone will take you back to see Dr. Berg."

By this point, he could pretty much fill out a standard medical questionnaire with his eyes closed. It was all the same. Surgeries and allergies. Insurance and history.

But there, at the very bottom of the page, was a single question he'd never been asked on any other form.

How much do you want it?

There was no box to check next to it. Not even a black line to write on. Just a clear call to hard work.

Luke's SEAL training instructors had asked him the same thing, and he'd showed them he wanted it more than anything else he'd ever dared to dream of.

"Almost done?"

He jumped at the feminine voice that didn't belong to Tara. The woman standing at the wooden door that presumably led to the exercise and exam rooms offered neither a smile nor a frown. Her face was simply relaxed. One hand rested on her hip, and she cocked her head, sending her long black hair over one shoulder. The collar of her navy blue polo shirt stuck up below her left ear.

At least she wasn't wearing a white coat.

Undoubtedly another of Dr. Berg's assistants.

He held out the completed form, and she took it, nodding down a short hallway. "We'll go all the way down to the big room at the end."

As he moved in that direction, her steps eerily silent behind him, he fought the rush of uncertainty that washed across his shoulders. Another set of soundless footfalls had taken everything from him. His palm slipped against the grip, suddenly slick and clammy, and sweat broke out across his upper lip.

This wasn't the same.

It *wasn't* the same.

How many times would he have to remind himself of that before he believed that he was home, that men didn't walk around with bombs strapped to their chests and women didn't push strollers of explosives down city streets?

He paused just long enough to swipe his forearm across his mouth.

"Do you wear out more easily than you used to?"

"Not much." That was a bit of a whopper, but he didn't feel like explaining that his sudden sweats had less to do with muscle strain and nearly everything to do with a memory he couldn't erase.

The hallway seemed as if it would never end, with her unseen, unheard steps always behind him. Finally he reached the open entrance she'd indicated. The room was bigger than his old apartment. There was a row of weight machines along the far wall and floor-to-ceiling windows to his left. The panes were covered with fabric shades, which kept the setting sun mostly hidden. To his right sat three consultation tables.

The woman leaned her hip against the first table, fixed her wayward collar and crossed her arms, her gaze assess-

ing and cool. When her stare hit his wrapped knee, she
lingered, and the muscles in his back grew tight. Even
with his sweatpants tucked into his brace, he felt bare,
too exposed.

"When will I meet Dr. Berg?"

Her wide eyes met his gaze, a frown pinching the corners
of her mouth. "I didn't introduce myself, did I?" He shook
his head. "I am Dr. Berg. Mandy. Please, call me Mandy."

His eyebrows shot up before he could stop them. So, this
was the good doctor. The young doctor. She looked just
about old enough to start college, but she'd helped Matt
more than three years ago. She wasn't exactly a rookie.

Clearing his throat, he tried to find something to say.
Nothing came to mind. Not even a generic greeting.

That was odd. He'd never been at a loss for words before the bomb. Before the surgery. Before his future had
become so absolutely uncertain.

After what felt like hours of weighted silence, she pasted
a smile into place. "So tell me, Petty Officer Dunham—"

"Luke."

"Excuse me?"

"Please. I prefer— Call me— It's just Luke." He bit
off the words, unsure how to explain that the medical discharge he'd been offered was one signature, one failed
physical away. And after that, he'd never be a petty officer
again. Every official document that touted it, every voice
that spoke it was just more evidence of how close he was
to losing it. All of it.

And a reminder of how much he'd already lost.

"Of course." She pressed her hand flat to her stomach,
her shoulders rising and falling in an exaggerated motion.
"How long were you at Walter Reed?"

He hitched his chin toward the manila file lying on the
table next to her hip. "Isn't that in my file?"

"It is. But I'm asking you."

He narrowed his gaze on her, trying to read between the smooth angles of her face, but whatever she was thinking was hidden beneath a mask of easy professionalism. She maintained eye contact, never flinching, even as he felt the scowl that had become his cover slide into place. "Too long."

She gave him a half smile, the corresponding jolt in his stomach making him stand up a little straighter. She should be frowning. After all, he'd perfected keeping people at a distance since the surgery. Keeping them at arm's length was easier than watching their pitying expressions.

"And in calendar terms?" she asked.

The muscles in his jaw screwed up tighter than a tourniquet. "Three weeks before they could move me to San Diego."

"Other injuries?"

He shrugged. "There were a few." *Dozen.* The shrapnel from the blast that had twisted his knee had left marks up and down the left side of his body.

But all of that would be in his file.

She nodded, flipped her hair over her shoulder and motioned to a padded chair. "Would you like to sit down?"

He studied her face, looking for any hint that she knew just how uncomfortable these crutches were. But her mask held. She didn't give him even a twitch of a smile as she nodded to the seat opposite her.

With a sigh, Luke lowered himself onto the chair, keeping his left foot a safe distance off the ground. His crutches clacked together as he slid them between the legs of the chair.

"If I take you on, you'll be with me three times a week for at least six weeks. And when you're not here, you'll be exercising at home. Most days, you're going to wish you were back in the hospital. It'll be awful. But after a while, it won't be."

"Wow." He fought the grin that threatened to find purchase and instead opted for a verbal jab. "Do you start every consultation with that sales pitch?"

"Only the ones that need it."

"Huh." Refusing to analyze what she was really saying, he got right to the point of his visit. "Will I be able to get back to my team?"

She squinted until one eye disappeared altogether. "That depends."

"On?"

"You…mostly." She patted her belly. "Are you strong enough? Will you listen to me when I say it's time to wait? And put in the work when I say it's time to go?"

He couldn't keep in a bark of laughter.

Something like a challenge flickered in Mandy's eyes, and she leaned forward. "We'd start out easy the first couple sessions. You've been out of the gym for more than a month."

"But before that, I was in the gym for half my life."

"Only half your life?" She shrugged her shoulder and pursed her lips. "What was that? Ten years?"

"It was long enough." A low sizzle in his veins demanded attention, calling him to prove her skepticism wrong. He crossed his arms, displaying some of the results of those years in the gym as he stretched the shoulders and sleeves of his gray T-shirt.

Thirteen years in the gym couldn't be denied. Nor could three years as a SEAL.

"I'm not so sure about that." She leaned forward, invading his space, and he pulled away, into the unyielding chair.

"Get used to it, Luke. We're going to have to get a lot closer than this if we work together."

But that was still a big *if*. He hadn't even decided if he wanted to work with her.

Except…

Well, there was something about her that reminded him of one of his instructors during SEAL training. Chief Willard had been hard and unflinching, smart and determined to see Luke succeed. And Luke had. Mostly because of the chief.

Could Dr. Berg see Luke through this new challenge?

"You look like you're in pretty good shape physically." An unspoken question washed over her face. *How did you stay so fit?*

"Force of habit."

"What is?"

"Exercising." His gaze drifted past her, to the shadow of a palm tree beyond the parking lot outside. It looked just like the trees visible from the Coronado beaches where the SEAL teams trained, and his heart jerked with an acute longing to be back there with his brothers.

"And your doctors at the hospital let you keep up a routine?"

He pinched his bottom lip between his thumb and forefinger, forcing his mind from sandy shores. "More like they ignored it when I didn't show signs of atrophy."

Her brown eyes glowed with something new, something interested. "What have you been doing?"

"Mostly resistance bands and bodyweight moves. Whatever I can do from my bed or a chair."

She took a long pause, crossing and uncrossing her legs, tapping her foot, running her fingers across her chin. All the while, her gaze never left his face, until he could physically feel her assessment.

The silence built like a concerto, its pressure pounding at his temples until she spoke. "I wish I could help, but I don't think I'm the right physical therapist for you. But I'll have Tara give you a list of other qualified, local PTs, who might be a better fit."

His heart flipped in his chest, disappointment raging

through him like a clap of thunder. "I thought this meeting was to help me decide if *I* wanted to work with *you*."

"You thought wrong."

Mandy bit the inside of her cheek to keep from smiling at the confusion splashed across Luke's boyish features. She felt bad for him. Really. But she was doing him a favor.

He needed someone who could really commit to helping him return to active duty. He might never return to the SEAL teams, but his service as a navy medic didn't have to be over. He deserved a PT who didn't require an extra arm's length between them.

And it had taken her all of five minutes with him to know that she'd have to keep him at least that far away. Farther would be safer. For both of them.

Besides, her future was a little too uncertain at the moment to take on a long-termer like Luke.

"So, you're what? You're passing me off?" For someone who hadn't looked very happy to be in her clinic in the first place, he sure sounded bitter at her rejection.

"It's best for you to have someone who can give you the time that I just can't right now." She tried to give him an encouraging smile, but for some reason it faltered. "If you want your old life back—"

He snorted. "Is that even possible?"

She eyed the brace around his knee, wanting desperately to make him promises. But she just couldn't do it. "Maybe."

"And those other physical therapists, are they as good as you are? Are they as likely to get me back out there?" His hand waved toward the beach.

A rubber band around her stomach went taut at the muted hope lacing every one of his words. Mandy opened her mouth to answer with the socially acceptable, politically correct response, but something about Luke's situation called for her to be honest. "They're good. And they can help you."

"Right." He clambered to his feet, his crutches clanging together as he hopped on his good leg, angling toward the hallway and the exit beyond. "Thanks for your time."

"Listen, Luke. I'm sorry."

He paused but didn't turn back toward her. "Sorry that I'll never serve on the teams again? Or that you're sending me to a second-rate PT?"

She crossed her arms, tilted her head back and took a cleansing breath, sending up a silent prayer for patience. "The most important person in your recovery is you."

She picked up the file his surgeon had sent over and flipped through it. Of course she'd already read it cover to cover—twice. But he didn't have to know that. For the moment, she just needed something other than his slumped shoulders and haggard features to focus on.

Beneath the prickly shell and tart words was a man in pain.

But she couldn't help him.

She couldn't afford to invest in a case like his. In a man like him. Not again.

When Luke reached the entry to the hallway, Mandy called out to him, "I really am sorry. Please ask Tara for some other names."

He didn't stop or even indicate that he'd heard her.

Luke was just too much like Gary. Too handsome. Too sharp. Too striking.

The very memory of Gary, who'd been her patient nearly four years before, sent shivers down her arms.

She couldn't think about him. She didn't want to. And Luke would be a constant reminder.

Pushing herself up, she marched down the hall and ducked into her office. The tiny room was a lesson in sparseness. The walls were white, save for three framed diplomas over a large wooden desk, which sat opposite two padded chairs. A stack of files in the in-box on the corner of her desk called for her attention, but the enormous bouquet of white roses in the middle of her workspace filled her senses. She pressed her nose into them, inhaling the sweet, clean fragrance. Like a spring rain, they washed away any uncertainty left over from her meeting with Luke.

She'd done right by him, sending him on his way.

"Tara, are you out there? Where did these come from?"

There was no response. Tara must have stepped outside. Digging through the satin-soft petals, Mandy found a card and quickly opened it. Patients often sent thank-you cards but rarely flowers. And who had known that white roses were her favorite?

Tugging the little green card from its envelope, she took another rich breath.

I miss you. I miss us. Gary

Nausea curdled the contents of her stomach, and she doubled over as bile reached the back of her throat. No longer sweet, the roses stank of betrayal and broken hearts and her very worst mistake. With a single sweep of her arm, she sent them flying over the edge of her desk. The glass vase hit the metal trash can with a crack loud enough to reach the parking lot, immediately followed by a shriek and rapid footfalls.

"Mandy?" Tara called before she even appeared in the doorway. "What happened?"

Mandy kept her chin tucked into her chest and her arms crossed. With shaking legs, she turned toward Tara. Her breath hitched as she tried to answer the question still hanging over the room, but there were no words to explain the pounding of her heart.

Tara remained silent for a long moment before finally

offering an uneasy chuckle. "Two bouquets in one day. That must be a record."

Mandy glanced up, not quite meeting her office manager's gaze over a small bouquet of orange-and-red lilies that she hadn't even noticed in Tara's hand. "An-other?" Her voice quaked, and she quickly cleared her throat, forcing her shoulders back and her head up.

"From Gwen." Tara held out the square vase. A tall plastic stem held a simple card, its looped letters easy to read.

Congratulations on your award! Well done, my friend!
  I've got a job for you in Miami whenever you want it.
Gwen

✂ "For the philanthropy award." Mandy spoke as though Tara hadn't read the card, which she certainly had. "You know. The one for my volunteer work at Pacific Coast House. I don't know how Gwen heard about it, but it was really sweet of her to send me such pretty flowers, wasn't it?" Mandy chomped down on her tongue. Why was she rambling as though she had something to hide? She wasn't a child in trouble. She was a woman capable of making her own decisions.

Tara nodded and raised an eyebrow, but her expression was otherwise blank. "And Miami? Are you thinking about moving?"

"No… Yes… Maybe." She ran a hand over her face and shrugged.

Tara's pale eyes turned hard, fearful. She probably thought she was losing her job, and Mandy jumped to clarify.

"Of course, I won't leave you out on a limb. I'll let you know as soon as I decide. It's just an offer. Gwen's a good friend from school, and she offers me a job in her clinic every year or so. I wasn't really considering it until…"

She couldn't find the words tonight. But Tara didn't really need her to rehash it. Her office manager knew about the identity theft, professional aggravations and general harassment Mandy had endured for almost two years. The cops hadn't been able to find anyone behind the hassles, but someone was out there. Faceless but intent on making her life miserable.

Maybe what she needed was a fresh start. And that was what Gwen offered.

She'd be a fool not to at least consider it.

And Gary's sudden return to her life—well, that was just another good reason to pack up and try again. In Miami.

"I promise I'm just thinking about it," Mandy said. "*If* I decide to go, you'll be the first person I tell."

The corners of Tara's mouth quirked into a half smile. "Fair enough." She tipped her head toward the front desk. "I'm going to take off. Need anything else?"

Mandy shook her head. "Have a good night."

She settled in to do some paperwork as the front door swished open and closed with the racket of the blinds.

Not a minute later, the blinds rattled again. Mandy jumped and then forced herself to laugh. "Tara? Did you forget something?" she called.

Silence was the only response. And it was quickly followed by goose bumps up and down her arms. Mandy stood and walked around her desk, then poked her head into the hallway, her pulse already accelerating. "Tara?"

Still no response.

Not a voice nor even the sound of anyone breathing. The office was deserted except for her. But something was different. Like the weight of a never-shifting gaze pressing against her shoulders. She jerked around, then looked the other way. No one.

Mandy tiptoed toward the front desk, the overhead lights in the reception area shining brightly. "Is someone here?" Her voice cracked as chilled fingers crept down her spine.

Peeking around the corner into the waiting room, she surveyed the space. Nothing out of order.

She shook her shoulders and cleared her throat. She hadn't really expected to find anyone. But what had shaken the front-door blinds? And why did everything inside her scream she wasn't alone?

Suddenly a car alarm screeched to life. Mandy jumped and clapped her hands over the scream on her lips.

Lights from the parking lot flashed through the front windows, and she dashed across the room, flicking the shades wide enough apart to peer into the darkness beyond.

The flashing and honking continued as a man on crutches hobbled along the side of the angry car. His back to her, he was bent as far as his supports would allow. But she didn't need to see his face to recognize him.

After unlocking the front door, she opened it and stepped onto the top step. "Luke? Are you okay?" Even her yell was hard to hear over the blaring horn, but he straightened up and spun to look in her direction. Holding his hand to his ear, he shook his head. He couldn't hear her.

She dashed across the empty parking lot, only then realizing how dark it had become. The lights in the lot were probably set on a late timer, and the moon wasn't doing much to break through the cloudy San Diego evening.

"Are you all right?" she asked when she reached his side.

Luke frowned and glared at the fast-food bag clasped against his hand grip. "I just walked over to get some dinner. I'm borrowing my mom's car—it fits my leg brace—but it's still not easy to get in and out of. Anyway, I accidentally hit the panic button on the key fob, then dropped the keys under the car." He rolled his eyes, his mouth pinching tight.

Mandy's heart gave a tiny hiccup.

Once he would have just crawled under the chassis and picked them up. Now he probably felt…helpless. He wasn't helpless. But to go from active-duty SEAL to needing help to walk couldn't be easy on a man, especially one used to patching up his wounded brothers.

Squatting down next to the car and leaning into the ear-splitting shriek, she spotted the keys, leaned against the abrasive asphalt and reached all the way under the car to retrieve them. Dropping them into his palm, she dusted off her hands as he pressed a button and the car let out one final honk before falling quiet.

Sweet silence hung in the air for a long moment before Luke cleared his throat. "Thank you."

She gave him a half smile and a quick nod. "Have a good night."

He didn't respond but angled himself toward her as she stepped away. His gaze was heavy on her back, sending even more chills racing down her arms. She picked up her pace, everything inside her suddenly jumping to high alert.

With a quick glance over her shoulder, she checked on Luke, who was still watching her. His features were pulled tight and unreadable.

A band clenched her middle, demanding she go back and talk to him. Go back and explain why she'd had to turn him down.

Halfway to the front steps, she turned around and called his name. "I really am—"

Squealing tires cut her off, and she jerked around to face the brilliant headlights of another car. It barreled down on her, picking up speed and stealing her every thought.

She tried to scream, but nothing came out.

The car was gaining ground, nearly to her. The driver had to see her. She was the only target in the vehicle's lights. And it didn't slow down. In fact, it was gaining speed.

Mandy managed a stumbled step as the car came faster and faster. Without a doubt she was about to die.

Suddenly an arm clamped her around the waist. It scooped her off her feet and sent her sailing out of the path of the car just as it careened by.

Mandy's wildly beating heart was firmly lodged beneath her larynx, which accounted for the lack of sound coming out of her mouth, even as she tried to scream. At some point in the previous half second, she'd clenched her arms around Luke's shoulders. And she had no intention of letting go.

"It's okay. You're all right." Luke's chest rumbled against her side as he spoke into her ear, the even rise and fall of his shoulders in stark contrast to her erratic panting. "It's gone. It didn't hit you."

Her breath caught on a hitch. "Or—or you?"

"I'm fine." His voice didn't even wobble.

How could he possibly be so calm when someone had just tried to run her over?

Someone had tried to kill her.

TWO

Luke blinked against the surge of adrenaline rushing through him. It was a familiar—welcome—feeling. It felt like all of his training. All of his missions. All of his past.

Pulling Mandy closer to his side, he eyed the single crutch he'd lost to the speeding car. One second slower, and it would have been his leg. Two seconds slower, and they would both be dead.

Clearly this was a new emotion for Mandy, who shivered against his side, her eyes blinking, unseeing. He patted her back awkwardly and cleared his throat. "You're good. No one was hurt."

He thought he was being reassuring, but when her eyes swung in his direction, they were filled with terror. "You're sure? You're not injured?"

Meeting her gaze, his lips twisted into a hint of a smile. "No more than I was an hour ago, Dr. Berg."

She gave him an obligatory chuckle, but the storm inside her danced across her face. "You just saved my life." It was almost a question, as though she needed confirmation.

He nodded. "A little bit."

That made her chuckle for real, and the fear he'd read in her eyes began to ease. "Look at me. You're practically carrying me." She untangled her arms from around his shoulders, her fingers from the spot where they'd burrowed beneath the collar of his shirt. Her warmth replaced by the cool breeze.

Luke dropped his arm, too, suddenly off-balance, and wavered dangerously. She flung a hand around his back and leaned a shoulder into his side as she eyed the mangled silver support left in the car's wake. The trashed remains of his dinner like a comet's tail.

"We came pretty close, didn't we?"

He didn't have to ask her for clarification. She could see only one thing, her focus entirely on what might have been. Instead of answering her question, he glanced over her head toward the office door. "Do you have an extra set of crutches in there?"

Her gaze dragged from the top of his head to the sole of his shoe. "Nothing that would be tall enough for you. But I do have a wheelchair."

Just the word made him cringe, but he finally nodded. "All right."

Leaning him against the railing, she said, "Stay here. I'll be right back."

Luke bit back the retort on the tip of his tongue. Where could he go?

But she didn't need a sarcastic comment after an ordeal like that. What she needed was to sit down for a little while to let the adrenaline subside and the trembling stop. And she probably didn't need to do that by herself.

The door opened with a bang, followed by the squeaking wheel of the chair she'd promised. She angled it down the steps, skipping the ramp altogether, and slid it to his side. "Have you been in one of these?"

"For a week or so. After the…" Man, it was still hard to say the word.

"Bombing?" she filled in.

He nodded and lowered himself into the chair, and

Mandy adjusted the footrest so his leg was propped out directly in front of him.

Patting his foot, she said, "There you go."

"Thanks. I'll get it back to you when I can get another crutch." He glanced toward his mom's car, and her eyes followed. Tight lines formed around her mouth as she bit her bottom lip until it was nearly invisible. "Are you going to be okay?"

She nodded, then her eyes grew wide. "But your supper is ruined. Let me buy you another hamburger. I'll even throw in a shake."

Luke squinted up at her, trying to assess how much of her offer stemmed from guilt and how much was from just not wanting to be alone. He almost asked her if there was anyone waiting at home, but even he knew better than to broach such a personal topic on their first meeting, no matter how close he'd been holding her just a minute before.

The flickering smile on her face dimmed for a split second, and he caught a glimmer of the terror she still battled. He'd faced down his share of angry terrorists—or tangos, as his team called them—and sharpshooters over three tours in the Middle East, and it never got easier. Mandy was a first-timer. Actually, she was holding it together pretty well, all things considered.

But she couldn't fully mask the fear. Her hands wringing and eyelid twitching, she maintained eye contact, but her smile never quite reached her eyes.

"It's the least I can do," she said.

Something in his gut promised his life would be easier if he just walked away. But he'd never walked away from *hard* before.

"All right. I'll let you buy me a double-double."

She pointed toward the glass door to her office. "Let me just lock up." She dashed up the stairs, her movements fluid and graceful. All four of his older sisters had taken ballet when he was a kid, and he'd been forced to sit through endless recitals. Somehow, watching Mandy's easy motion reminded him of those hours.

Jealousy surged deep in his belly. He might never move that freely again.

He'd always been so stable on his feet. So sure of his footing. Now he needed a shoulder to lean on just to stand.

Getting back on the teams was a pipe dream. At best.

So what was he supposed to do with all of the free time suddenly laid out before him?

The lights inside the office flicked off, and an instant later, Mandy exited, locking the door behind her. Shoving her keys into a small tote bag, she flipped a wild curl out of her face. With little more than a smile, she led the way across the lot to the sidewalk and then down to the light so they could use the walkway.

She didn't say anything as they crossed the street, but her foot hesitated as she checked each direction three times before setting out. He pushed his chair behind her, the muscles in his arms aching at the new movements. He was panting by the time they reached the far side of the street, sweat trickling down the back of his neck.

At this rate, he didn't belong anywhere near the SEALs.

Inside the crowded red-and-white diner-style fast-food joint, she got into line. "What's good here?"

"You're from San Diego, work right across the street, and you've never been to an In-N-Out Burger?" Luke couldn't keep the snicker out of his tone.

Mandy shrugged one shoulder before turning back to the menu board. "I'm from Colorado."

"Uh-huh." That explained nothing. Maybe she was a health nut who refused to enjoy the greasy goodness of the Southern California staple. Luke was all for fitness. All for staying in good shape. He was also one for enjoying a stack of steaming beef covered in melting cheese when the day called for it.

And a near hit-and-run definitely called for it.

His stomach rumbled at the smell of the best burgers on the West Coast.

"Your options are pretty much a burger or a burger and fries," he said.

She shot him a snarky grin, but ordered a burger and fries when she got to the counter.

They found an empty table, settled in and were halfway through their dinner before he came up for air.

Mandy stared, her gaze unfocused, at a glob of ketchup on her fries. She hadn't done more than pick at her burger, but she didn't seem eager to chat.

He didn't really want to start a conversation, but something about the tightness of her chin—as if she was trying so hard to hold it still—made his chest hurt. "You want to talk about what happened back there?"

Her gaze shot up, and she looked surprised to see him there. "I'm sorry. I was just… I guess I just zoned out for a second. What did you say?"

"Back in the parking lot—" He tipped his head toward her office. "That wasn't an accident. You want to talk about it?"

As the words rolled out, he knew he meant them. It was more than idle curiosity. He was tired of being unproductive. Maybe he could help her. Talking about it might help her deal with the experience.

He hadn't had a mission in weeks. And he was months away from another. Just the idea of giving her a hand brought the side of his mouth up in a smile.

"Um. No. It was nothing. Just an accident, probably."

Nope. That wasn't true.

Her gaze jumped to the left, then down at her hands in her lap. Her shoulders squirmed, and she bit the corner of her mouth. She knew it wasn't an accident or a distracted driver. Someone had intentionally tried to kill her.

"I doubt it." He shrugged as if they weren't discussing life and death. Perhaps if she didn't think about what was on the line, she'd open up about it. "Who'd you tick off? Someone not get the results you promised?"

Her nostrils flared, and her eyes narrowed. "I didn't tick anyone off, thank you very much. I'm a professional, and there are no guarantees in medicine."

The bright pink spots in her cheeks were so cute that he couldn't help but goad her a little more. "Come on. You can tell me. What'd you do? Break too many hearts?"

Her gaze fell to the table, where she twisted a straw wrapper into smithereens. Forehead wrinkled and neck stiff, she let out a tiny sigh before squaring her tense shoulders and forcing a half smile. Another chink in her armor. But she was determined to keep from showing it to him.

His middle jerked with regret. "I'm sorry. I shouldn't have pushed." He stabbed a hand through his shaggy hair while she still looked anywhere but at him. "You're in trouble." He didn't ask a question because it would have been too easy for her to deny it again.

After three years on the teams, he couldn't walk away from someone in need.

He'd never been able to. That was why he'd wanted to be a SEAL in the first place. That was why he wanted to go back.

"I've got it under control." Her chin didn't so much as quiver, and she met his eyes with a steady gaze.

"What else has happened? Is this the first time someone's tried to run you over?"

"Nothing's happened." She shook her head, but her eyes lost a hint of the mettle that had just been there. "Everything's fine. I've got it under control."

He'd believe that when the stars quit shining. "Have you talked to the cops?"

She nodded, looked away and toyed with a French fry, dunking it in ketchup before using it to doodle on her burger wrapper.

Apparently she had it under control, but she had still gone to the cops. She was scared. She was in over her head. And she was a sitting duck.

"What are the cops doing?"

"A detective is looking into it."

"Into…" He let his voice drag out, hoping she'd fill in the blanks because there were still a lot of them in her tale.

Brown eyes, narrow and uncertain, met his gaze, and he could see the battle just beyond them. There was more to tell, but she barely knew him.

Someone had threatened her life, and opening up about that wasn't easy.

Luke hadn't talked to anyone except the navy chaplain about the suicide bomber who had nearly blown off his leg. And Bianca, of course. Back when she'd been his girlfriend. That conversation had started with him laying it all out on the line—an uncertain future, months of PT, maybe never returning to active duty—and had ended with her walking out of his life for good. After that, he hadn't talked about his leg, even with his swim buddy and best friend, Will Gumble—Willie G. to his teammates. Putting his pride on the line was riskier than walking through a minefield, so it was easier to just keep it inside.

Except the memories gnawed on his insides like a hungry dog, leaving him raw and sore.

Whatever haunted Mandy probably warred within her, too. To talk about it or not to talk about it. It was a lose-lose situation.

Mandy crumpled her hamburger wrapper around the last bite, her stomach suddenly not at all interested in fin-

ishing the meal. There was something else chewing at her, an urge to tell Luke what was really going on.

His gaze dipped to her hands, and he watched her fingers work the crinkling paper into a ball for a long second. "You don't have to tell me anything that you don't want to. I get it. I've been there."

"I'd guess you're still there." The words popped out as soon as she thought them, and she clapped a hand over her mouth.

A wry grin curved the corner of his lips, and he shrugged one shoulder. "You might be right. Looks like we have more in common than we thought."

Maybe it was the knowing spark in his eye or the understanding in his tone. But something made her snap, the truth—all of it—spilling out before she could overanalyze the reasons why she should keep her distance.

"About two years ago, I realized that my identity had been stolen. Nothing that a thousand others haven't dealt with. Credit cards taken out in my name, debt racked up. That kind of thing. I reported it to the credit bureaus and law enforcement, but it just seemed to get worse. And then someone tried to hijack my professional license."

Luke's eyebrows pulled together, but the rest of his face remained even. A slow nod encouraged her to continue.

"I only caught that because it was time for renewal, and I had turned in my paperwork a bit early. Two days later they received another renewal with my name but a different address."

"And that address…"

"Was a fake." Mandy put her elbows on the table and leaned a little closer to Luke so she could keep her voice low. "It's like there's a phantom after me. No name, no address, no face. They're always three steps ahead of the police."

"And they're doing a pretty good job of making your life miserable."

Her gaze snapped to meet Luke's. "Yes."

He narrowed his eyes, the skin above his nose wrinkling. "And…"

"How did you know? That there's more?"

"Identity thieves don't usually jump to attempted murder in one leap."

Murder.

The word made her tremble, and she closed her eyes, only to find headlights bearing down on her once again. Gasping a strangled breath, she looked up just as his hand rested on her fist. Jerking away, she squared her shoulders and forced her back ramrod straight.

Yes. That had been attempted murder just an hour before. She knew it. So did he.

"Why do you think the two are connected?"

She inhaled deeply through her nose and exhaled, like she perpetually told her patients to do. "Someone's been in my home."

His mouth dropped open. "Did you report it?"

"I couldn't. I didn't have anything to report." The questions in his eyes didn't require words, so she continued on. "It wasn't a blatant breaking and entering. Nothing was broken or taken. But things were moved, just enough to let me know that someone's been in there."

"What are you doing to protect yourself?" His voice was firm, almost demanding, and his broad shoulders stiffened. Suddenly his boyish face turned stern, strict. "It's not safe for you to be there alone. Not if someone is getting in and out without trashing the door or breaking windows."

She offered him a half smile for his concern. "I know. I had an alarm system installed as soon as I realized something was off. The alarm hasn't been triggered, and my stalker hasn't been back."

"Who else knows the alarm code?"

"Just the guy who installed it."

Mandy gave herself a mental pat on the back as Luke's muscles began to relax, his clenched jaw easing into a more natural expression. She was doing everything she could do to keep herself safe.

"Have you thought about a dog?"

Well, almost everything she could do. "I'm allergic."

"Who's watching your six?"

"My six?"

"Your back. In the SEALs we don't go anywhere without a buddy. You can't see behind you at your six o'clock, so you need someone who can." When she didn't immediately respond, he gave her hand a gentle nudge. "Do you have family nearby or a good friend?"

"I…" Her voice trailed off as a coolness settled over her. "My family is all back in Colorado. And we're not very close, so when I came out here for school, I just stayed."

"A friend, then?" His eyes were filled with hope as deep as the Pacific, and she wanted more than anything to give him the answer he was looking for.

She shook her head. "It—it takes a lot to get a business going. I have friends at Pacific Coast House—"

"Ashley Waterstone," he interrupted, a little grin spreading across his face. "She made me come to see you."

"I know." Mandy pursed her lips to the side at the memory of Ashley's call. She'd been nearly as intimidating as her six-foot-two SEAL husband when she'd told Mandy that she had a friend in need of help. Mandy just hadn't planned on the man sitting across the table from her, his crooked grin and boyish charm a little too disarming. A little too much like Gary's.

She'd made the right decision turning Luke away.

She had.

She was certain.

Almost.

Luke's head bowed as his shoulders rose and fell in an even rhythm. He almost looked as if he was praying, until he glanced up without moving his head. "I think we both know that Ashley, Staci, Jess and the others at Pacific Coast House can't afford to get mixed up in this situation. They have families to think about."

His tone was filled with as much compassion as she'd heard from him, but it didn't take away the sting of his words. The truth of them. She pulled her hand from where it still rested beneath his and hugged her arms around her middle.

She was going to have to face this alone.

Do not be afraid.

The words rang through her, true and clear, and she knew in that instant that she could face whatever was coming.

His mouth quirked to the side. "Of course, that wouldn't stop them. I get the feeling they like you a whole bunch."

A tear tried to force its way out, and she blinked it into submission, swallowing the lump in her throat. "I like them, too. And I'd never ask them to put their families in danger for me. I can do this. On my own."

He tapped his long tan fingers on the table where her hand had been, and she suddenly missed the reassurance of his touch. But the warmth in his eyes wrapped around her heart.

She could face this. Whatever it was. Whoever it was.

"So here's the thing. Those ladies, they're like my big sisters. And their husbands, they're my bosses and friends. If I let anything happen to you, I'm pretty sure they'd take out my other knee." He chuckled at the half joke, but the truth about his injury kept his jaw tight.

"What are you saying?"

He shrugged. "I'm available."

She knew what he meant, what he was offering. She just wasn't ready to give him an answer. Accepting him meant allowing him into her life, and her track record with that had led to her very worst mistake. Even if this wasn't a romantic relationship.

But refusing him left her out in the open, unprotected. Neither was a good option.

So, instead of responding to his offer, she asked a question of her own, forcing her smirk back into place and hoping to make him squirm. Just a little bit. "Are you trying to ask me on a date?"

Without missing a beat, he winked and replied, "Whatever it takes to keep you safe."

With a shake of her head and a low chuckle, she sighed. He was far too charming for his own good. For her own good. But his proposal was too important to ignore. "Don't you have something better to do?"

"As a matter of fact, I don't." He thumped the brace on his leg. "I'm supposed to be resting my knee when I'm not in physical therapy. My life is looking pretty dull from where I'm sitting."

"A SEAL without a mission…"

"About the worst hand a guy could be dealt." There was truth in his tone, a longing in his voice to return to a life of significance.

Except…well, she wasn't sure a guy in his condition could keep her safe.

As soon as the thought crept in, she laughed it away. He'd saved her from a speeding car while using crutches and carrying his dinner. And he'd kept his cool the whole time. He was capable, even with his injury.

But letting him help her also meant allowing a man back into her life. It meant being reminded of another relationship that had turned sour, that had turned her into someone she hated.

Do not be afraid.

She could handle this. She *would* handle this, by setting up the boundaries from the start.

"Just so we're clear, I was joking before about you asking me out." He raised an eyebrow in question. "There'll be no—" she waved her finger back and forth between them "—dating."

He winked again, that saucy grin falling back into place. "Whatever you say."

Her stomach swooped and tightened, and she leaned toward him, needing him to understand, to agree. "That's a nonnegotiable. I don't date patients. Period."

Both of his eyebrows went up this time. "So, I'm a patient now?"

She was as surprised as he looked. When had she decided to take on his case? She hadn't. Not consciously anyway. But...

"I suppose so. I spend most of my time at the office, and if you're going to be around, you might as well be getting your feet back under you."

His smile turned from playful to appreciative. "I won't let you down."

She wasn't going to overanalyze whether he was referring to her situation or his healing. Either way she was stuck with him now. At least it would be on her terms. "All right. But no dates." His Cheshire grin never wavered, and she had a sinking feeling that his flirting was going to play a prominent role in their relationship.

It was worth it.

Because maybe, just maybe, he could help her stay safe long enough to figure out who was trying to kill her.

THREE

Mandy spent the entire night before Luke's first appointment calling herself every name in the book. She was a special kind of crazy to take him on. If she had half a brain, she would have found a way to put as much distance between them as she could.

Except she hadn't had a choice.

And his eyes had spoken volumes across the table two nights before. He could help her. And as much as she didn't want to need him, she did. The exact kind of professional help he could offer.

But the more she thought about having Luke around, the more she recalled the other man in her life. The one who had wormed his way into her personal life and into her home. Who had made her miserable.

Chills raced down her arms, and she hugged her knees into her chest, pushing away all thoughts of someone else being in her house.

Suddenly being alone was too much, and she threw back the covers on her bed and ran for the bathroom. Slamming and locking the door behind her, she got ready in record time. Her hair was still damp as she raced down the road to her office.

She skidded into her regular parking spot on the side

of her building and ran through the nearly empty lot, past the scene of the would-have-been hit-and-run.

When she reached the glass double doors, they were already unlocked. She hesitantly ducked her head inside until Tara waved at her from behind the desk. "Morning, boss."

"Hi, Tara." Mandy slipped the rest of the way in, wrestling her overstuffed tote bag through behind her.

"You're in early today." Tara's grin sparkled as though she knew a big secret.

Mandy covered a yawn with the back of her hand. "I didn't get my paperwork done last night." There. That was a very valid excuse for running away from her own home.

"Su-ure." Tara singsonged the word as if she knew more than Mandy gave her credit for.

"And I need you to pull out an inactive file. I took on a new client."

Tara's eyebrows rose, her forehead wrinkling as she steepled her fingers beneath her chin. "Oh." Again, that knowing tone. "Do tell."

"Dunham. Luke Dunham."

With a low cackle, Tara pulled his file from a stack on the side of her desk. "I had a feeling we hadn't seen the last of him."

"It wasn't… I… Things changed."

"Uh-huh." Tara tapped the point of a pen against her tongue before scribbling a note on the chart. "First appointment?"

Mandy hated the guilt that tumbled within her. She still owned this practice. She was still in charge. So why hadn't she told Tara about Luke's appointment until today?

There wasn't time to dig into her real reasons for it, and if she let the conversation go any further, she'd have to explain to Tara about nearly being hit by a car and someone breaking into her home. Better to keep this conversation short. "Four o'clock. Today. I'll be in my office until my first appointment arrives."

The rubber soles of her shoes squeaked against the laminate flooring as she kept her stride even and unhurried. She had no reason to run. At least not from Tara.

The day passed like a minute, each patient taking all of her focus, deserving all of her energy. It was after three when she finally looked up and realized she hadn't eaten anything since the banana she'd snatched on the way out the door that morning. Her stomach growled loudly as she marked another patient's progress in his chart.

With a quick sweep of the exercise room, she confirmed that the only other occupants, a teenage girl working on a balance ball with one of Mandy's physical therapy assistants, hadn't heard her body's retaliation for not feeding it. Stretching her back and shoulders as she stood, she headed for the front office to see if there were any leftovers to be had.

"Haven't seen you all day." Tara didn't even look up from the computer where she navigated complex medical-charting screens that fed to area hospitals. "I thought you were avoiding me, boss."

"I was." Mandy laid the sarcasm on thick, and Tara glanced up just long enough to offer a smile.

"Hungry?"

"So much. Anything good back there?" Mandy peeked down the hall toward the office kitchen. It was a tiny room with a round table big enough for only two chairs. The counters boasted only a coffeemaker, sink and a toaster oven. Even the fridge looked as if it belonged in a dorm room rather than in an office.

As Mandy slipped toward the break room, Tara scrambled out from behind her desk, the wheels on her chair clacking against the tiled floor as she ran to catch Mandy.

"So are you going to tell me what happened with the SEAL?"

Mandy frowned as she eyed a half-eaten salad and a tray of veggies left on the counter. A wilted piece of roast beef squished between two slices of bread sat beside the tray, the last in what had been a plate of sandwiches. The soggy bread and warm meat looked as appetizing as congealed gravy. Someone had ordered in, and she'd missed the invitation.

Rats. Now she was going to have to face the SEAL in question on an empty stomach.

"He has a name, you know." Mandy plopped several pieces of limp lettuce onto a plate before digging her fork into it.

Tara nodded. "I do. But if the rest of his team had any intelligence, they would have nicknamed him Adorable."

Mandy snorted so hard, she nearly choked on her bite. Quickly swallowing the offending mouthful, she was about to respond when the bell on the front door rang, and Tara dashed to man her post.

She'd just taken another bite when Tara called down the hallway, "Mandy? You have a visitor." Her words were stilted, hesitant, as though she didn't really want to say them. And they turned leaves of lettuce into gravel as Mandy swallowed.

Setting the plate on the table, she tiptoed down the hallway, poking her head around the corner just as the bell above the front door jingled again.

Luke appeared at the entrance. The setting sun behind him left him in shadow, but she could still feel the weight of his gaze as he maneuvered his new crutches through the door.

"Luke." Her voice went higher than she'd expected, and she quickly cleared her throat. "You're early."

"Thought I'd bring back the chair you let me borrow."

"Thanks."

Suddenly someone else cleared his throat. It was low and tinged with mild annoyance, as if he'd been put out by her short exchange with Luke. Mandy didn't really need to look at him to identify the visitor Tara had announced.

He was tall and broad, his dark hair still falling over his forehead, no matter how many times he pushed it out of the way. His smile still ticked up to one side, but where it had once been charming, now it was smarmy, turning her skin to gooseflesh at first glance. His eyes were deep brown, but they lacked any compassion or understanding of the part he'd played in her greatest regret. And now they shot from Mandy to Luke and back, filled with questions.

But she didn't owe Gary Heusen any answers. In fact, she had plenty of questions of her own.

"What are you doing here, Gary?"

He held out a bouquet of roses. More white roses. More reminders that he'd once known her and claimed to care about her.

Her heart picked up speed, and a bead of sweat formed on the back of her neck, trailing below the collar of her shirt. She pressed a hand to the wall for support, hating her body's reaction. Hating that she couldn't control the way she responded to the memories and that the broken heart he'd left behind suddenly felt all too fresh.

"Luke, why don't I go with you to get the wheelchair?" Tara's voice broke the trance in the room, but Luke scowled at the idea.

"Are you okay, Doc?" While he clearly addressed Mandy, his eyes narrowed on Gary, a warning written across his features.

"I'm fine. Please, would you go with Tara? I can handle this." She could. She would. Forcing her shoulders square and her back straight, she watched Luke follow Tara out of her office.

When the door closed, she turned on Gary in a hushed but firm voice. "What are you doing here?" she repeated. "I don't want you here."

Gary's eyes looked in the direction of the path Luke had just taken. "So you've replaced me?"

Anger shot through her like a volcano, unbridled, untamable. "What are you talking—"

Two voices from down the hall suddenly joined them, and Mandy clamped her mouth closed, trying for a stabilizing breath. "We can't do this here."

"Then let's go to your office." He tucked the flowers back into the crook of his arm and held open the wooden door to the back hallway. She didn't have any choice. She knew he wouldn't be going anywhere until he said whatever he'd come here to say.

Marching down the hall, she led him to her office. The minute he was inside, she spun on him in a hushed growl. "You have two minutes. This better be good."

The cool assurance on his face dimmed for a split second, before he amped up his toothy smile and held out the flowers. "You're as pretty as ever, Dee."

"Don't call me that. I don't like it," she said, crossing her arms over her chest.

"You used to."

No, I didn't. But this was not the time to argue with him. "Get to the point. What do you want?"

He twisted the bouquet in his hand, showcasing his empty ring finger. "A lot's been going on lately."

The last time she'd run into him, Gary had been wearing a gaudy gold ring, a symbol of his marriage. The one he hadn't bothered to tell her he was about to enter while he wooed her. The one she hadn't asked about. Mandy pinched the bridge of her nose and pressed her other hand to her hip.

"I'm not interested in playing your games. I have a busy day, and you don't need to be here."

"Don't you understand? Camilla and I aren't together anymore. You and I can finally have a future."

"What?" She shrieked the word so loudly that everyone in the building probably heard it.

Gary reached for her hand, but Mandy jerked away, shaking her head. "Camilla knew," he continued. "She knew that I always loved you best."

"Love? Is that what you call it?" Mandy gave up trying to keep her voice low, her tone even. This man was crazy if he thought she'd have anything to do with him after what he'd done. "Lying to me? Leading me on? Breaking my heart? That's love?"

"Baby, it was you the whole time." He gave her his best smile, and it succeeded only in making her stomach turn.

"Listen to me very carefully. You're not welcome here. I don't want your flowers. I don't care what happened between you and Camilla. I don't want to see you again." She took a step in his direction, hoping he would back up, but he didn't, and suddenly they were closer than she wanted.

His smarmy grin turned just a little bit cruel.

How had she ever fallen for his act, for the facade? Oh, he'd been a good actor, for sure. Attentive. Interested. Caring. And she'd wanted to see those qualities in him. She'd wanted to believe the best in him so much that she'd ignored every warning.

Except he'd done it all to feed his own ego, to prove to himself that he still had whatever it took to win a woman's heart. But after the winning, he'd been more than happy to crush it. And now that she knew it, it was easy to see in every facial expression, easy to hear in every word.

"Oh, you'll see me around," he said. "You forget we have ties to the same circles."

"What circles?"

"The Pacific Coast House carnival fund-raiser is next week."

"You wouldn't." She narrowed her eyes and pressed her hands to her waist. "You've never cared about anyone as much as you care about yourself. You wouldn't show up at the carnival."

"Sure I would." He let the flowers drop to his side, still holding her gaze. "And Camilla might be there, too."

"Why? She has no connection to PCH."

He shrugged one shoulder beneath his dark brown leather jacket. "She always said she didn't like you. Maybe she thinks you're the reason our marriage fell apart." He turned on the charm as if he'd flipped a switch. "Of course, I know that's not true. We were doomed from the start. She has a terrible habit of lashing out when she's angry."

A scene from Mandy's waiting room four years before flashed through her mind, and her insides twisted like a screw. Camilla's eyes had been wild with rage, her motions fierce. She had knocked over chairs and broken a lamp and left the office in disarray. Gary had sworn she wasn't normally like that. When she was on her medications.

Mandy covered her mouth with her hand, her breath suddenly short.

If she wasn't taking her medications, Camilla was prone to lash out. Like trying to run someone over.

A brick settled on her lungs, and Mandy fought to speak. "Is she taking her meds now, Gary?"

He shook his head. "I'm not sure."

"Okay. You need to go now."

Gary opened his mouth to refuse the request, but instead of his voice, another one filled the room. "You heard the doc. It's time for you to go."

The guy Mandy had called Gary took one look at Luke—even on his crutches—gave a silent nod, tossed the flowers on Mandy's desk and ducked out of the room. The bell on the door declared his exit from the building.

Luke kept his distance from Mandy, trying to read her face, but she'd put a mask on, all professionalism. "Let's get to work." She marched past him and down the hall toward the exercise room. She pointed to the closest exam table. "Hop on up."

He bit back every question racing through his mind and did as she said, letting her have this moment of control.

When he was settled onto the table, she rested her hands on his back. Even through his T-shirt, they were like icicles, and he jumped.

"Sorry." She blew on her palms and rubbed them together until they whistled at the friction. "Go ahead and lie down. Let's get this brace off and see where your range of motion is at."

He did as she instructed while she began loudly peeling back the Velcro strips. "Lift your leg." She helped him raise it just enough to slide the brace out of the way. He felt a hundred pounds lighter and also as if he might fly apart given a stiff breeze. The knee brace had been his companion since the surgery, and without it, he was incomplete.

"All right. Really carefully, we're going to bend your knee." She put her hands around his calf and pulled gently.

He inhaled sharply. His leg felt as if it would split into two pieces. Like a freight train running him over, the pressure against the stiffness was more than he could handle. He pinched his eyes closed and brought a fist to his mouth.

"Good. You're doing really well." Mandy's tone was soothing and calm as she straightened his leg and then bent it again.

"Are you trying to tear my whole leg off?"

She laughed. "No. But this *is* your first appointment. You never know about next time." On the fourth pass, she said, "Think about something else. What did you think about when you were in SEAL training?"

"About how much I wanted to be a SEAL, but now…" He let the silence that followed finish the thought. He didn't have to say it. They both knew that now there were no assurances. There was no certainty that he'd ever be on another mission with his SEAL brothers.

Nothing was a guarantee. No matter how much he'd begged God to heal him, to give him a new knee, he hadn't heard anything from above.

But he did have a mission now. His assignment was Mandy's safety. And he could think on that.

"So, are you going to tell me about the guy in your office?"

"No." There was no humor in her response.

"Okay. What about the Camilla woman? Sounds like she might be holding a grudge."

Mandy kept her hands gentle, but her tone firm. "Maybe."

"What happened with her?"

"I don't know."

Luke frowned at her.

Even though she kept her gaze firmly locked on his knee, she said, "I only met her once."

"Then why would she have it out for you?"

"She thinks I tried to steal her husband."

Something strange and altogether unwelcome roared inside him, but he couldn't call it by name. It burned like anger but not quite. It twisted his insides like bitterness, only not as strong. It was indistinct but demanding.

One thing he knew for sure. Mandy hadn't stolen anyone's husband.

He'd known her barely three days, and he already knew she wasn't capable of such a thing.

"Why does she—" He groaned as she bent his knee farther than it had moved since Lybania. Since the explosion.

Mandy didn't bother to apologize, but she did give his quad muscles a gentle massage. "You're going to be a little stiff tomorrow, but it'll be the good kind of sore."

After a few more minutes, she reached for his brace.

"Already? I can do more." He swiped his arm across his upper lip, wiping away the sweat that had pooled there, even from such a light workout.

"I know you can. But you shouldn't." Helping him sit up and swing his legs back over the edge of the table, she looked right into his eyes. "I have a feeling half of your battle is going to be just letting it rest. The surgeon didn't repair your medial collateral ligament. That's only going to heal with rest. So you have to take it slow."

He leaned into her until their foreheads were only a couple inches apart. She smelled of hand sanitizer and citrus, and he offered her a compromise. "Then you've got to give me more to work on than the first name of a woman you haven't seen in years."

She reached for his crutches and wedged them in front of her. "You need to rest."

"And you promised to let me help you."

She lifted her eyes toward the ceiling as though asking for patience from above. "I don't have anything else to give you right now. I'm going to call Detective Fletcher, who I reported the almost hit-and-run to, and tell him what Gary said so he can look into Camilla. And then I'm going to go home."

"At least let me walk you to your car?"

A slow smile lifted her cheeks, despite the shadow of fear reflected in her eyes. "All right."

He trailed after her as she went to her office and called the detective. It must have gone straight to voice mail, and she left a short, succinct message. "This is Mandy Berg. I have a tip on someone who might be taking her frustrations out on me. Would you call me back as soon as you have a chance?" She gave him her number before hanging up. Then she tossed the flowers, which were still sitting on her desk, in the trash and scooped up her tote bag. "Let's go."

"Good night, Tara," Luke said as they walked through the lobby.

"Have a good one," she hollered over the sound of her radio, which was playing a hit from the mideighties.

Luke clattered down the ramp beside Mandy, thankful she hadn't suggested taking the stairs. "Is everything all right at your house? No one's tripped the alarm?"

"It's all fine. Nothing new since two nights ago." Her eyebrows furrowed. "Well, nothing except finding out about Camilla."

"Do you think she's capable of this?"

Mandy dug her hand into her bag, rooting around for her keys for several seconds before producing them. "I don't know. I don't know her. But a woman scorned, well, she's capable of nearly anything."

Luke nodded as the lights on her white SUV blinked. He glanced at the wheel as she opened her door, and the parking lot lights reflected off a puddle peeking out beneath her front bumper. "I think you're leaking."

"I know." She threw her bag into the car and slid behind the wheel. "It's been leaking antifreeze for a couple days. I need to have it looked at."

He nodded. "You've had other things on your mind." He put his hand on her door to close it. "Have a good night. Drive safe."

"I will."

The door clicked closed, and he stood silently watching her pull out of the lot and onto the major cross street. When she had disappeared, he moved toward his car, watching the pool of liquid in her empty parking spot to make sure he didn't slip in it.

The yellowish lights above made the puddle's color hard

to distinguish, but it wasn't a neon color like many anti-freeze brands. In fact, it looked more like oil.

A knot in his stomach went taut, and he shifted one of his crutches to the other side so that he could bend almost all the way over. Stretching his arm as far as he could reach, he swiped a finger through the fluid. Dry and oily. Lifting it to his nose, he inhaled. It smelled like fish oil.

Like brake fluid.

Like her brake lines had been cut.

"Mandy!" He yelled her name, even as his throat closed. The strangled cry died quickly on the wind, and he ran as fast as his crutches would carry him to his car.

Get to her. Get to her. Get to her.

He had to find her before she couldn't stop. Before she sailed through a red light or flew off a mountain road.

He flung his crutches into his car, gritted his teeth against the eruption in his knee when he bumped his leg and peeled out of the parking lot. He whipped in front of another car and floored it in the direction she'd gone.

She hadn't given him her cell number. Too personal.

But this, this was beyond personal. This was a matter of life and death.

FOUR

The light before the highway entrance turned yellow, and Mandy pressed her brake pedal.

Her car barely slowed and coasted through the red light, accompanied by the angry honking of several other drivers. Her SUV let out a squeal of pain. With white knuckles, she gripped her steering wheel and tried to pull over, but there was no shoulder and she was moving too fast. A car at her side blocked her in, and one in front of her slowed way down.

"Please. Please. Please," she begged as she pressed her sluggish brake again. Her car gave a woeful shudder, stopping just inches from the bumper in front of her.

"What's wrong with you?" Leaning back, she glanced at her floor mat, which seemed to be bunched under the brake. Giving the carpet a tug, she pressed the pedal again. Her little SUV lurched but stopped.

Much better.

Even so, the interstate's stop-and-go traffic could be more than trying if her brakes were being cranky. With a quick turn, she slipped into another lane. She'd take the back roads home. Dark and windy, but at least they weren't quite as busy.

Mandy zipped along the twisting roads as she headed up the hill, hugging the center line, keeping her distance from the sheer cliff to her right. The vertical wall of stone on the far side of the two-lane highway was almost invisible against the black sky as she worked her way out of the city. One pair of headlights in her rearview mirror and the fading red lights of three other cars in the distance before her were her only company.

She let out a breath, already feeling the stress of the day and Gary's visit lifting.

Until she tapped her brakes as she crested a summit.

Nothing happened.

She punched them hard and gasped as the pedal reached the floor. With no response.

Grabbing the wheel with two shaking hands, she tried to keep her vehicle in her lane as it picked up speed.

The road before her curved back and forth, a black snake—and just as terrifying.

Blood rushed in her ears, swallowing every other sound, including the frantic prayer leaving her lips. "Help me. Please. I need help."

The car behind her seemed to be gaining on her, but she couldn't let herself be hypnotized by the white lights. Her lane seemed to narrow, and she focused on the center line.

Just stay away from the edge. Don't go over. And don't miss a turn.

Her palms turned slick, but she couldn't risk wiping them. Mandy squeezed the steering wheel tighter, praying she wouldn't make a wrong turn. The road had to level out. It had to.

But it just continued its steep decline. No escape. No emergency exit.

Emergency.

Her emergency brake.

She grabbed the handle next to her seat and pulled it as hard as she could. It refused to engage. The red light on the dashboard didn't even appear. The rapid-fire beating of her heart drowned out everything except the truth. Someone had cut her brake lines and disabled her emergency brake. Someone wanted her to go off that cliff.

The same person who had tried to run her over.

Suddenly the headlights in her mirror barreled down on her, almost reaching her bumper before swinging up beside her.

She couldn't make out the car or the driver in the dark, and he swerved closer. As if in slow motion, she waved him off, but he just drew nearer. Was he trying to push her over the edge?

She wouldn't give him the chance.

Leaning into the steering wheel, she swallowed the lump in her throat and pressed the gas. Her car gained a little ground before her pursuer caught up. His whole car seemed to be shaking with the effort to maintain the speed, but he kept his distance from her, hugging the far line as he whipped down the opposite lane.

Risking a glance in his direction, she caught a waving hand and a familiar mane of shaggy blond hair.

Luke.

He motioned for her to roll down her window, but did she dare risk taking her hand off the wheel again? But what did she have to lose? She was dead either way.

With one flick of her finger, the window automatically went down. Tears filled her eyes at the wind's unrelenting assault.

"Emer—cy. Bra—"

The howling wind seemed to steal his words, but she tried to respond. "Broken!"

He didn't reply. Maybe he hadn't heard her. She tried again but stopped short as a set of headlights glared right at them.

"Car!"

Luke shook his head and cupped a hand to his ear. Forgetting all about her sweaty palms, she jerked a hand in the direction of the truck heading right for him. At the same moment, the other driver leaned on his horn.

Suddenly Luke was gone. Vanished as the truck careened past her, still honking his displeasure. But all she could hear was the *no, no, no* that crashed through her mind.

She craned around as much as she could without losing sight of the road and caught a glimpse of the car behind her, just as the road swung wide. Overcorrecting for it, her back wheel caught the yard of gravel at the edge of the incline. The back end of her car whipped to the left. Then dangerously close to the cliff. Her heart stopped.

This was it.

She was going over.

Suddenly she was back on the road, her speedometer pushing ninety.

She wanted to cover her eyes or hold her breath or do anything to keep from seeing her inevitable end.

Lord, let this be quick.

"Run—way. —uck. Ramp!"

Luke had returned to her side, and he pointed just to her left.

A brown sign pointed to a gravel runaway-truck ramp. It was going to total her car. And maybe her body. It was also her only hope.

Heart in her throat, she jerked the wheel toward the exit, praying that she hadn't chosen the wrong way out.

Gravel crunched beneath her tires, the momentum of the car sending her flying forward.

And then it all slammed to an end.

Luke skidded to a halt at the base of the ramp, grabbing his crutches and leaping from the car before it had fully stopped. He set the foot of his injured leg down, immediately regretting the decision. "Ahhh!" Fire shot through his knee at even the lightest pressure, but he swung his way toward the cloud of dust masking Mandy's SUV. When he reached the rear bumper, he tossed his crutches down and used the vehicle to keep his balance as he hopped toward the driver's door.

There was no sign of movement from within, and Luke forced his voice to remain steady as he called out. "Mandy? Doc? Are you okay?"

She didn't respond, and he hopped a little faster, matching the rising tempo of his heartbeat. He hadn't thought it could go any faster than it had when that truck had come flying around the curve and he'd had to slam on his brakes. He'd whipped behind Mandy only a fraction of a second before the big rig would have slammed into him.

But the thought of what he might find inside her car had his heart hammering a painful tattoo.

"Luke?"

The voice was no more than a breath, and he thought he'd imagined it until he hopped another foot in her direction.

"Luke? Are you okay?"

The sudden quiet in the center of his chest echoed through his limbs, and he closed his eyes to capture the memory of that peace. "Fine. I'm fine. You?"

There was a long pause. He couldn't move fast enough to get to her door. Finally his fingers wrapped into the open window, and he pulled himself even with it, staring hard through the muddied air.

Large brown eyes blinked twice before closing for a long moment. Her pink lips formed a tight line as though she was trying to pull herself together before speaking. The rest of her face was painted in a fine layer of grime.

He reached for her cheek, but stopped short. She hadn't moved any of her limbs yet, and he wasn't about to touch her before he knew how badly she was injured. "Can you move your arms and legs?"

Without opening her eyes, Mandy waved both hands and bounced both of her knees. A soul-crushing groan followed.

"Where do you hurt?"

"Everywhere?" She swung her head in his direction, and only then did he see the streaming red line above her right eye.

Shrugging out of his long-sleeved overshirt, he pulled it inside out, wadded it up and pressed it against the gash. With his other thumb, he swiped at the dirt on her cheeks, looking for other abrasions. "You hit the steering wheel?"

She started to nod but seemed only able to manage a grimace. "How bad is it?"

"It could have been a whole lot worse."

She opened her eyes at that. Fear and something close to panic lurked in the depths there. They were on the same page. She'd dodged another bullet, another attempt on her life. But someone was more calculating and brazen than they had guessed. Whoever it was had access to Mandy and her car. And he wasn't going away.

After clearing her throat, Mandy reached up for the shirt pressed against her hairline. Their fingers brushed as she felt around for the right angle, and he was tempted to give them a comforting squeeze, until she took charge. "I've got it."

"Honestly, how much does your head hurt?"

Without missing a tick, she replied, "Four out of ten."

He'd guess from the size of the gash and speed she'd been going, she was more likely at a six. So she either had a high tolerance for pain or a low tolerance for letting people help her. Probably the latter. Doctors were notoriously bad patients.

"Do you have a flashlight?"

Rooting around in her center console, she finally pulled out a roadside-ready light and handed it to him.

"I was going to check your pupils—" he chuckled, pointing it at the ground and flicking it on "—but I think this thing would make you go blind."

"I'm all right. Maybe a mild concussion, but I don't have any nausea or ringing in my ears. And my head really only hurts right here." She tapped the shirt still stemming the flow of blood on her forehead. "I didn't lose consciousness, and I have no memory loss."

"Clearly you remember all of your concussion training from school."

She squinted sternly at him, but a tiny smile broke the facade. "Yes. I'm fine. How did you know to follow me? How did you even find me?"

"That puddle under your car wasn't antifreeze. It was brake fluid. I had a hunch you'd skip the highway if your car was acting up, so I chased you down. Hope you don't mind."

Her grin managed to reach another level. "Thank you."

"You're welcome." He nodded and leaned back enough to get a better look at her car, the tires nearly submerged in the sand. "You're still sinking. If you can move, we better get you out of here and call CHP."

The California Highway Patrol wouldn't be too happy that their truck ramp had been used by a smallish SUV, but Luke had never been so glad to see a ramp as he was that night.

Swinging her door open, he hopped on his good leg and offered her a hand to help her out of the car. When she landed on the shifting rocks, she stumbled against the car. Resting against its frame, she took several cleansing breaths.

"Dizzy now?"

"Just a little bit." When she opened her eyes, she reached for his arm but stopped short. "How did you get over here?

You can't be walking on your own." Her voice rose in volume and pitch with each word.

He nodded toward the crutches leaning against the bumper. "I just hopped the last eight feet."

Her narrowed gaze homed in on his face. "Do you have any idea how badly you could have reinjured your knee? Sand, gravel, anything like this—" she stomped her foot on the yielding ground "—could mean the end of your full recovery. The end of your chances with the teams."

Her words hit just where she'd aimed, like a punch to his gut and a left hook to his jaw, for good measure. But he didn't look away, even as he tightened the muscles keeping his injured leg elevated. "I wasn't thinking. I saw your car slam to a stop, and…" His voice trailed off as he waved a hand toward his car, its headlights illuminating them from the base of the ramp.

Mandy scrubbed her free hand down her face and rubbed at her eyes. "Thank you. Thank you for…" She finally looked away, long lashes shading the storm in her eyes. "Thank you for following me. For checking on me."

The rush of fulfillment that always came in the middle of a mission surged through his veins, and he smiled at her. "I'm glad I was there."

"Me, too. But promise me that you won't be careless."

He hopped several times and twisted to pick up his crutches—making sure his knee was completely out of danger—shooting her a wry grin in the process. "Why, Doc, you sound like you really want to see me pass my navy physical."

"Of course, I do." She began a slow, careful descent, passing him with ease. "I hate wasting my time."

By the time they asked CHP to check for any evidence Mandy's attacker had left behind on her car, said good-bye to the officers and arranged for the wrecker to pick up her vehicle, Mandy was ready for a hot bath and a full night of sleep. Neither seemed plausible, though. Even if she could get into a bath, she was pretty sure that she hurt too much to get out of it. And every time she closed her eyes, she felt that sickening lurch of her tire catching on the gravel, nearly flinging her off the road.

"Do you want me to take you to the ER to get that checked out?"

She jolted at the nearness of Luke's voice, right next to her in the car, then groaned as she cradled her left arm across her chest.

Everything. Hurt.

And that ache was beginning to surpass the stinging on her head. Flipping down the visor of the passenger seat in his car, she opened the mirror and pulled the shirt back to reveal the wound. The hair right above her forehead was matted and brown, but the red stripe wasn't oozing. She prodded it with a tentative touch. "I don't think so. It's not very deep. I just want to go home and get some rest."

"Classic head wound." Luke carefully positioned his injured leg below the steering wheel and closed the driver's side door. "Those usually bleed like they're going to kill you, even if they're just a scratch." He followed the motion of her hand with his eyes as she pulled her fingers away to confirm the bleeding had stopped.

The tips were clear, save for the dirt caked in every knuckle and embedded under every nail. She looked as if she'd been in war rather than simply doused in sand and grime. Maybe she could swap the bath in favor of a hot shower.

When she was clean and rested, then she could face whatever—whoever—was out there.

"Where am I going?"

She pointed him down the hill in the direction of her house, thankful for the telltale jerk as he tapped his brakes, pulling back onto the deserted highway. Still, her heart beat just a little harder with every swerve in the road and change in the slope.

They sat in silence for several minutes, her eyes glued to the edge of the reach of his headlights.

"You want to talk about it?"

"What, exactly?"

He lifted his right shoulder and dipped his head to the far side. "I don't know. Anything. Like when you knew you were in trouble. How you're feeling." A hitch in his voice suggested that he wasn't any more eager to talk about her feelings than he was to lose the brakes in *his* car.

Good.

She didn't want to dissect the emotions rolling over her wave after wave, like the never-ending Pacific surf. There were too many of them, and trying to pull them out and analyze them left her chest aching for air and her eyes stinging with unshed tears.

No matter how involved in her situation he had become, Luke was still her patient. And she had to keep some semblance of distance between them.

"Or about who might have sabotaged your car."

Sabotage. Somehow that was a much safer topic.

"I don't know who's after me."

He pulled off the mountain road onto a city street and stopped at a red light. Her seat belt pulled snugly across her chest, and she gasped as it set off a chain of mini explosions. Groaning as she hunched forward, she squeezed her eyes closed against the pain where she had slammed into her own seat belt not even an hour before.

"What about that guy at your office today?"

"Gary?" she asked, even though there was no question who he was talking about.

Luke nodded. "You never finished telling me about him and Camilla."

And she didn't have any plans to. Ever.

Instead she steered the conversation into safer waters. "Until a few days ago, I just thought someone was trying to make my life miserable. I could believe that someone would be angry enough to steal my identity and try to get my license suspended." She'd been staring out the window but turned to stare at him when she asked, "How crazy does someone have to be to try to kill another human being?"

A muscle in his neck twitched, his gaze never leaving the road. His jaw worked in slow motion, as though he was chewing on his words before speaking.

Her insides did a total flip, and a boulder filled her throat. Had she really just said that to a navy SEAL? To someone who had undoubtedly been on the shooting end of a gun and maybe even on the receiving end of a bullet? Yes. Yes, she had. This was not safer waters.

"I am so sorry. I didn't mean that."

The corner of his mouth tipped up into a crooked grin. "I know what you meant. I've seen this kind of thing before."

"Cut brake lines?"

"Crazy people."

Somehow, despite the constant ache in her midsection, throbbing at her temples and her foot lodged firmly in her mouth, she managed to match his smile.

"I got this knee a couple weeks before the end of my third tour. That was more than enough time to see some crazy. Like men who kidnap and threaten aid workers." He glanced her way, and she turned toward him, leaning into his story. But he stopped cold.

Mandy's friend Staci Sawyer had been a prisoner in Lybania only a couple years before, detained for passing out Bibles while running a clinic for women and children. Had he been part of the SEAL team that rescued her?

"Staci?"

His lips pursed to the side, and she knew he wasn't going to confirm. He didn't have to.

"Listen." The timbre of his voice dropped as he pulled into her neighborhood. "It's not easy aiming a gun at another person. It's certainly not easy to pull the trigger. But I made peace with God about that a long time ago. What I do isn't about greed, ego or passion. I do it to protect as many innocents as possible. But some people are just looking for revenge or so filled with hate that they can't see beyond their own pain. Those are the ones you've got to watch out for."

"That's my place." She pointed to the small blue bungalow in the middle of the block.

He pulled up to the curb and parked the car, but Mandy made no move to get out.

After a long pause, she asked, "How do you know who to watch out for?"

"The ones who cut your brake lines *and* disable your emergency brake—within steps of your office—those are the dangerous ones. Those are the ones who think they have nothing to lose."

FIVE

As Luke smacked the rubber heel of his crutch against the front door of the clinic, he caught only a glimpse of Mandy across the lobby. If the bags beneath her eyes were any indication, she hadn't been sleeping very well since the car accident four days before. Flushed cheeks and an unusual shuffle in her step revealed her exhaustion, but she disappeared down the hallway before he could call out to her.

Tara sat behind the counter, her face pulled tight as she watched Mandy walk away.

"Tell my next patient I'll be ten minutes." Mandy's voice barely stretched into the reception area, and it carried a note of weariness. Tara opened her mouth to respond, but the door swung shut behind Mandy.

"She doing okay today?" Luke asked as he signed his name to the sheet on the clipboard.

"Only if semi-comatose is considered okay." Tara shrugged, and he cringed. "She's running on autopilot. Has been for a few days."

Luke pursed his lips and stared at the closed door as if he could see through it, see what was really going on in Mandy's mind. He wanted to know, needed more information to begin to help her. But he didn't have any idea how much she'd told Tara. He couldn't begin asking personal questions if Mandy hadn't shared anything with her office manager.

Instead he leaned an elbow on the counter and turned up the wattage on his smile. "So, tell me. What's a guy got to do to make her smile?"

Tara's grin slowly grew. "Depends. What are you thinking?"

"I don't know. Something to let her know she has a friend. Flowers?"

With a quick shake of her head, she stopped that train. "Her favorites are white roses."

The memory of Gary's bouquet and Mandy's pained expression when she'd seen them made the back of his throat burn. Flowers were definitely out.

"Does she collect anything?"

"Diplomas."

He snorted. He'd seen the impressive lineup of degrees displayed on her office wall. "Listen, if you think of something…"

Tara scribbled something on a sticky note and tucked it into the beach bag at her feet. "I'll think about it and let you know."

He tipped his head toward the bag. "Been going to the beach?"

Her gaze darted in the same direction, and she nodded quickly. "I like the solitude. I'm always looking for the perfect spot, just a quiet place to read." She reached down and pulled out a dog-eared romance novel before tossing it back into her bag.

"I miss the water. Just the sound of it."

Tara's mouth turned into a strange frown, and Luke cleared his throat and laughed. No need to get quite so sentimental. He'd get to go back someday. Just not until his knee was fully healed.

And maybe not for any more training.

"Before I officially started the SEAL program, I used to go to this beach all the time to run a couple miles. It's a pretty narrow section of surf, but the shore felt like quicksand on my boots." Just the memory of those runs made his legs ache. "But there are rocks surrounding it, so it's not great for surfing. I was usually the only person out there."

Tara sat up a little straighter. "Really? It was empty?"

He shrugged. "Most of the time. Especially in the evenings."

"Sounds right up my alley." Her smile revealed a previously hidden dimple, and her eyebrows disappeared under the orange fringe of her bangs. "I don't suppose you'd want to share your secret hideaway with a fellow beach lover, would you?"

"Sure." After all, if he couldn't use it, someone should. He scribbled a few directions on a sticky note. "It's north of Mission Beach but not quite to La Jolla."

Tara's smile began in her eyes. "Thanks."

"Tara, is Luke here?" Mandy's voice filled the entire office.

"That's your cue. Do you need help with the door?"

"Nope." He leaned awkwardly on one of his crutches and clambered through the opening with a belated word of thanks.

The empty workout room greeted him at the end of the hall. He'd passed Mandy's office, but her door had been closed. He did a slow, clumsy circle just to make sure he hadn't missed her.

Sure enough, she stood in the corner closest to the hallway, her back flush against the wall, hands flat on either side of her legs. Her khaki pants looked as if they'd spent a week crumpled up on her bedroom floor. Her lips were drawn tight, and the color he'd seen in her cheeks before had vanished. Her eyelashes fluttered as she opened them, managing a wan smile in his general direction, but she didn't make eye contact.

He moved a step in her direction. "Mandy, are you— You don't look very—"

"Good to see you." Her tone said it was anything but. "Hop on up on the table and take your brace off."

"Doc?"

She grabbed an exercise band from a wooden peg next to the wall of windows. "We're going to do some more stretching, and I'm going to show you a couple exercises I want you to do at home this week."

He didn't get on the table. Didn't take off his brace.

Instead he stared at her. Hard. "It's just the two of us here." He dropped the volume of his voice a notch. "You don't have to pretend with me. I was there. Both times."

"I don't want to talk about it." She turned away from him, putting her shoulder between them like a wall.

"Are you sleeping at all?" Pressing a hand to her back, he leaned in.

She jumped at his touch and jerked away. When she swung around to meet his gaze, her eyes flashed with something close to anger, but it was mingled with terror. "I said—" her voice lethal "—I don't want to talk about it."

Luke dropped his hand to the grip on his crutch and took three steps back until he could lean against the exam table. Letting his foot rest on the floor, he crossed his arms and waited for the shock on her face to wear off. But she just stood there, her eyes wide, eyebrows raised and mouth open.

He fought the grin that wanted desperately to sneak into place. Her outburst was a good sign. An indication that she was healing. He'd much rather she lash out at him than keep her pain bottled inside.

But she didn't need to think he was laughing at her, so he bit his lips until he got the urge under control.

After three slow heartbeats, Mandy slapped a hand over her mouth and shook her head slowly. Her big brown eyes never blinked, and he could read every regret there. "I'm sorry." A muscle in her neck jumped. "I didn't— I shouldn't have spoken—"

The slightly wicked grin he'd been fighting before disappeared entirely, replaced by a warmth in his chest and a desire to protect this woman. Arms still crossed, he bent at his waist and gave her an encouraging nod.

"I'm just—" One of her hands fluttered about her head. "There's so much… Sometimes it just feels like too much. And I promised I'd volunteer at the Pacific Coast House fund-raiser this weekend."

The carnival. When Luke returned from his tour early, his best friend, Will, had invited him to go to the event in support of the shelter for women who had suffered domestic abuse. There would be a bunch of SEALs there, and Luke had zero desire to face them while still on crutches. Even if he couldn't ever rejoin their ranks, he could choose when he'd see them again. And it was not going to be hunched over and weak.

Completely unaware of his drifting mind, Mandy still chattered away. "But I can't even drive home without totaling my car. It's all so out of control. I mean, not just the car. And then he called, and all I can think about is what if he's right. And my patients deserve better than half of my mind, but I'm so distracted all the time. And…" She looked around, apparently only then realizing she was still rambling. "And I'm still talking."

He raised an eyebrow. "Well, you clearly had something on your mind."

"I suppose so. But you don't deserve to be yelled at like that."

"It's not the first time I've been yelled at." She blinked

slowly, confusion crossing the features of her face. "SEAL training isn't exactly kindergarten."

That was the understatement of the century. Those weeks had been filled with mental and physical demands like he hadn't imagined possible. All while being chastised by an instructor who had thought Luke was the weakest link in the class.

Yeah, he could handle a little frustration from Mandy. And he'd do so with a smile.

At least he had a mission. An assignment.

He'd get her through this.

"I'm sorry."

"Because you yelled at me or because my instructor did?"

She dropped her hands from her face, and a tiny dimple appeared in one of her cheeks. "Both?"

"Don't even worry about it. I'm here for whatever you need. We're in this together. If you need to blow off some steam, do it. You're not going to get rid of me that easily."

Twisting the exercise band in her hands, she nodded. "Thank you."

"So, tell me what set you off. You said someone called. Who was it?"

Who was who?

Mandy blinked rapidly, trying to rein in her wayward thoughts, which seemed intent on skipping down a path that was clearly off-limits. But when Luke had so adamantly pronounced that he wasn't going to leave her to face this all alone, her insides had done a little cha-cha. And suddenly the baby face under unruly whiskers didn't seem quite so young. Suddenly he wasn't a kid or nearly as unassuming as he sometimes seemed.

When he wasn't saving her from hit-and-run drivers, rescuing her from runaway cars or letting her yell at him, he came across as just another easygoing kid. Except there was an intensity in his eyes, and right now it was making her feel… Well, she wasn't quite sure what it was making her feel.

Or at least, she didn't want to give those feelings a name. They weren't safe, and they sure weren't professional.

"Doc?"

Her stomach lurched, and she pressed a hand over it, wishing she could control her response when he called her by the nickname. None of her other patients had latched on to her title like that, and she'd never really let them call her anything but Mandy. Only, Luke wasn't like her other patients. In fact, he wasn't like any man she'd ever met.

"Who was on the call?"

The call. Right.

She'd much rather think about his grin, or the way his eyes burned with a passion for life when he looked right at her.

But pretending she hadn't received it wasn't going to change the facts. With a deep breath, she closed her eyes and dipped her chin before meeting his gaze again. "The detective—Fletcher—called just a minute ago."

Luke's eyes narrowed, and his jaw tightened. He said nothing.

"He can't find Camilla." Even her name tasted bitter. "He said she hasn't been keeping her regular schedule. She hasn't been at work, and she's missed picking up a prescription refill."

"Prescription?" he asked.

"Gary—" just his name gave her a full-body shiver "—said she's been on medication that keeps her from having violent outbursts. But she might have stopped taking it."

"How violent?"

"Enough to trash a waiting room."

"Enough to try to run you over?"

"I don't know."

A silence hung over them as realization settled in. Camilla was the most likely culprit, and no one knew where she was or her next step.

Luke uncrossed his arms, the muscles in his forearms bunching as he pressed his hands to the table. "A few days ago you said she thinks you tried to steal her husband. Why would she believe that?"

The words were at the back of her throat before she could help it, but Mandy clamped her mouth shut to keep them from spilling out. The back of her eyes burned, and she tilted her head back and blinked rapidly.

It would be so easy to answer him, to confess to her own stupidity. After all, what kind of fool fell in love with an engaged man, a man who was a liar and a cheat?

But if she started, she might tell him all of it—the whole, terrible truth. The part that still broke her heart. The part she still saw and hated every time she looked in the mirror. Even after she'd suspected Gary wasn't free to love her, she'd stayed with him. Even after friends had warned her that he was in another relationship, she hadn't pushed for answers. She'd loved him and wanted him to love her so much that she'd turned a deaf ear to reality.

And she'd hurt Camilla in the worst possible way.

Telling Luke about Camilla meant also telling him her worst mistake. And that was something she absolutely could not do. That crossed too many professional boundaries. She was already in dangerous territory with him. He knew more about her current situation than anyone besides her best friend, who had just moved to the other side of the country.

Luke knew where Mandy lived. He knew how to protect her. And she was starting to rely on him.

Oh, she was in deep.

The wall had to start here. Now.

At least Gary had taught her that. There was no going back when the line had been crossed.

No matter how appealing Luke made it seem.

With a sad smile and a slow shake of her head, she pointed to the exam table. "Hop on up. We need to get to work."

Luke looked as if he was going to argue, but he stopped short, acquiescing with a little jump. The gray padding on the tabletop dipped under his weight and squeaked as he scooted into position. After rolling up his workout pants over his brace, he peeled it off, letting out a small sigh of relief.

With a grin, she put her hands around his calf, massaging her fingers into the muscle there. "That better?"

He nodded. "Sometimes that brace feels like it's made out of sandpaper."

She ran a finger down the skin next to the elevated scar that ran across his kneecap. It was healing nicely. Time to step up their routine. "You're going to wish you'd never taken it off today."

Thirty minutes later, Luke turned to her. "Why do you hate me?"

She laughed as she pointed to the parallel bars that ran the length of the far side of the room. One end had a full-length mirror for patients learning to use prosthetic limbs. Luke had been lucky. He didn't need that. But that wasn't going to make the first pass any easier. "Walk the bars."

He looked down at the new knee brace she'd given him. This one allowed him some mobility but still kept him from overusing the healing ligaments. "I'm not sure."

"Then it's a good thing I am." With a hand on his back, she propelled him across the room. The slow clack of his crutches sounded like a countdown, but she wouldn't let him fall. "You can do this. And I'll walk with you."

Luke shot her a dubious look. "And what? Get squished when I fall on you?"

"Give me more credit than that. I wouldn't let you walk if you weren't ready. But we'll still take precautions."

His forehead wrinkled when she held up a blue gait belt and leaned forward to wrap it around his waist. But he didn't say anything as she cinched it into place, giving herself something firm to hold on to should he take a tumble.

When he was set to go, she set his crutches aside and stepped up behind him. Almost pressed against his back, she slipped her hand between his shirt and the belt. The top of her head reached just past his shoulders, and she gasped. He was taller than she'd thought. Bigger. Broader.

Without the crutches, he was like a tower, his muscles defined beneath the lightweight knit of his T-shirt. The shirt was damp with his sweat from the strain of the simple stretches. Still he fought on. He didn't know how to quit. He knew how to push through the pain, his shoulders square and chin up. Even the stubble along his jaw didn't look so fair from her angle over his shoulder.

Yes. The kid was definitely gone.

And the zing of physical awareness running through her at this knowledge was entirely unwelcome. But not at all unpleasant.

With a tap on the outside of his left thigh, she said, "Pick it up. Little step."

He did as she said, every muscle in his back tightening as he set his foot down.

"Now the other. Little step."

The knuckles on his hands turned white around the silver bars, and his arms trembled almost imperceptibly.

She kept one hand at the belt and placed the other on his arm. "You're ready. Trust your knee."

"I'm not sure I know how." His voice was low and steady but filled with uncertainty.

"I won't let you fall."

"I'm not worried about falling."

Of course. The bunching triceps peeking out from below his sleeves could hold him up against the force of a hurricane. He was worried about relying on the leg that had let him down.

"If you can't trust your knee, then trust me."

Without a pause he picked up his uninjured leg and slid it forward. His breath hissed through clenched teeth, but he didn't wait to be told to take another step. With each shuffle, his muscles relaxed a fraction, yet the back of his neck glistened under the effort it took to keep moving forward.

She loosened her hold on his arm, and he paused, glancing over his shoulder just long enough to make eye contact.

Did he feel it, too? That strange energy that seemed to pass between them? Her attraction rolling off her in waves?

"How did you know I was ready?"

She shrugged. "It's my job."

"Thank you."

She gave him a saucy wink. "Funny. You only say that at the end of a session. I'm pretty sure you hate me five minutes into every one."

Looking straight ahead, he finished the route and then did a quick turn in her arms. Her hand still gripping the gait belt stayed put, and he was suddenly in her arms. When he looked at her, his eyes were alive and his face glowed.

She'd done that. She'd given him this moment of triumph. Being a part of this healing process had always been God's plan for her. She'd known it from childhood. But she'd let Gary and Camilla make her doubt her calling.

No longer.

She had a purpose here, and she was going to help Luke find his, too. Even if it wasn't on the teams.

"Are we going back?" He looked past her shoulder, his eyes locking on the far end of the room.

"Not today."

A frown tugged at the corners of his lips. "I can handle it."

"Without a doubt." She patted his side once before snatching his crutches. "But it's the first time you've used that knee since your surgery. And you've got to take it easy."

"Right. *Easy.*" The word sounded as if it tasted of brussels sprouts and vinegar, but he nodded his consent. "Can I walk around my house? No stairs."

She picked up his chart and scribbled a few updates. "No."

"But I just made it across the whole room."

"On bars." She kicked the metal, and it rang out. "You were leaning on these pretty heavily." He opened his mouth to interrupt, but she held up a hand. "That's what you're supposed to do. That's why they're there. But you don't have bars at home. And if you were to trip or fall, you'd risk another injury. A permanent one."

He glared at the ceiling, as if begging for patience. "Then by Friday?"

She looked at his chart to confirm the date of his next appointment—Wednesday—and the one after that. "We have to reschedule. I won't be here on Friday."

His eyebrows were almost so fair that they disappeared under the weight of his frown.

"I'm working the ring-toss booth at the Pacific Coast House fund-raiser."

His frown eased a fraction. "Right."

"Are you going?"

"No."

His sudden, definitive response struck a surprising blow, and she wrapped her arms around her middle at the sudden shiver.

Gary had threatened to be there. Camilla, too, maybe. Of course, Mandy wouldn't be alone. Ashley and her husband, Matt, would be there. Staci, Tristan—another SEAL—and their daughters would be working the dunking booth. Honestly, the place would be swarming with SEALs and their spouses, not to mention all of the other PCH volunteers.

But knowing Luke wasn't going to be there—well, it left her feeling like a ship without a port.

In the middle of a storm named Gary.

"Oh." She managed just the one syllable in a whisper before her throat closed up and her imagination carried her away.

"The guys will harass me to no end if I show up on these crutches. I was kind of saving my big return for when I'm walking on my own." He stopped speaking, his gaze intensified and he leaned in a little closer, studying her every expression. She tried to look away, to hide whatever he saw there, but he was too quick. "What are you worried about?"

"It's no big deal."

He reached for her hand and ran his thumb over her knuckles, leaving a trail of goose bumps in its wake. "Everything is a big deal until you're safe."

She shook her head. She didn't need him there.

Except maybe she did.

"Do you think Gary's going to be there?"

She nodded, hating the way her chin trembled.

He scratched the side of his face but never looked away. In fact his gaze only grew more intense. "Then I'll be there, too."

SIX

"Did you see who showed up?"

Mandy jumped at the voice in her ear, spinning to face her friend Ashley, bumping into her stomach. Immediately she reached out to rub the baby bump Ashley cradled in her hands, but this was no time for apologies. "Who?" Her stomach twisted at the face her mind immediately conjured.

Gary had all but promised he'd come. And there was no telling who or what he might bring with him.

Her gaze darted from tent to tent, searching out any sign of a threat among the throngs. Nothing seemed to be out of place, but what if she wasn't looking for the right things? Danger could lurk in any booth, behind any smile.

This could be the night her stalker found his mark.

Goose bumps rushed down her spine as a lump lodged in her throat, and she squeezed her friend's arm.

Ashley's blue eyes lit up as she nodded down the make-shift fairway. Past the man handing out whispery cotton candy to wild-eyed children. Beyond the booth with the blue-and-white-striped tent, where children threw balls at stacked bottles and squealed in delight when they hit the mark. Through the crowd of men lined up for a shot to dunk the most senior SEAL in attendance.

Mandy's heart lurched with relief, her breath releasing on a heavy sigh.

Where she'd expected to see Gary, she found Luke, all compassionate blue eyes and baby-faced grin. He locked onto her like a missile, weaving between friends and strangers alike but never stopping.

Ashley gave her shoulder a little push. "I'll watch your booth. Go see him."

"Who?" Oh, dear. She sounded far too innocent. Even she didn't believe her ignorance.

As only a true friend could, Ashley offered a sardonic glance. "You should talk to him. He's cute."

"You're married." Mandy tried to sound affronted, but she'd never been able to keep a straight face in the midst of a joke. When she broke, laughter bubbled out of Ashley.

Rubbing a hand over her belly, Ashley said, "And very happily so. But I'm not blind. I know a good man when I see one."

She wasn't wrong. Luke was a good man. And good-looking, too.

He was also her patient.

But there was no time to argue that point as the subject of their conversation arrived. "Ashley." He nodded to the petite blonde. "How are you feeling?"

"You sound more and more like my doctor every time I see you."

"And you still avoid answering my questions every time I see you."

"Touché, Cub."

Mandy chuckled at their exchange but paused at the unfamiliar nickname. "Cub?"

It was hard to tell for sure in the colorful lights winding up the tent poles, but Luke's neck seemed to turn pink. "It's nothing."

Ashley didn't have the same sense of restraint. With an evil grin, she began the story. "When he was in BUD/S—

that's Basic Underwater Demolition/SEAL training—he was a little chubby."

"I was not." He caught Mandy's eye, embarrassment pulling his features taut. "I was very average. I just wasn't as fit as some of the beasts in my class. And your husband has a big mouth."

Ashley rolled her eyes. "Anyway, with a round face, he looked like he was twelve. And he was endlessly polite."

"So they deemed you a Cub Scout."

Luke crossed his arms. "You're the first person to get that right away."

Mandy covered her mouth and the giggle that threatened. It wasn't a far stretch to see him as a little boy. After all, she'd viewed him that way for more than a few days. But no longer.

"My work here is done," Ashley said. With a quick squeeze of Mandy's elbow, she disappeared into a sea of smiling faces.

Without taking his eyes off her friend's retreating form, he stabbed long fingers through this hair, sending unruly curls in every direction. "Well, that was…"

"…sweet." Mandy filled in his blank but at his frown knew she'd picked the wrong adjective. "What? I think it's a cute story."

"Just what every SEAL wants to hear. Do me a favor?" He leaned in as if he was going to tell her the secret of Pandora's box. "Don't let any of the others hear you say that."

"Deal."

Just then, a little girl with blond pigtails ran up to the booth, waving two orange tickets. "I want to win!" Mandy handed her three green rings and showed her how to toss them at the metal bottles. The first ring landed on the ground three feet from the closest bottle. The second just a foot closer.

The girl's lower lip pouted as she fought back tears. "I was going to win that bear for my mommy."

Then Luke was at the girl's side, his big hand encircling hers. "Together?" He cocked his head to the side while she looked all the way up into his face. Whether she saw the kindness there or felt the restraint of his grasp, she nodded furiously.

They practiced the motion twice, and he whispered, "On three. One." Her eyes grew bright.

"Two."

Mandy held her breath.

"Three."

As if it knew exactly where it belonged, the ring sailed through the air in a perfect arch, landing on the nearest bottle. The girl let out a cheer of delight, clutching the bear that Mandy handed her as though it were priceless. She was gone in an instant without even a thank-you, but Luke's grin was witness to what they'd done.

"Nice work." Mandy had to stop to clear the lump in her throat. "You made her night."

"Then we're even."

His wink was nearly her undoing. Entirely enjoyable shivers ran down her spine, and she almost reached for his arm. She had to think about something else. Anything else. "You're on your crutches tonight."

He gave each of them a comically long perusal. "That is accurate."

The urge to make contact finally won out, and she risked a playful push on his shoulder, instantly regretting it. How could such a small exchange make her insides line up to do the conga? "I meant, it's going to be a long night on your feet. You could have used a wheelchair."

"I could have." His expression said it had never even been an option. Of course, he'd admitted that he didn't even want to meet his teammates while on crutches. It would be ten times worse to do it in a wheelchair. "But I have this annoying physical therapist who's always trying to get me to keep my muscles strong."

Her heart fluttered at his teasing smile, and she shot back at him as good as she got. "You're my worst patient."

He shook his head until one of his blond curls fell in front of his eyes, and he brushed it away with an easy flick of his wrist. "You mean, because I put all your other patients to shame."

"Something like that." Another playful push into his unmoving arm.

Teasing wasn't crossing the line. Was it?

No. They could laugh and joke. It was a natural part of a working relationship. It didn't mean anything.

Even if her physical reaction to his proximity wasn't quite on board with that.

"Are you really going to stay on the crutches all night?"

"As long as you're here."

He was so matter-of-fact about it. There was no doubt or question in his voice. He wasn't asking her permission or her approval. He was a man on a mission.

And apparently she was it.

Nothing had ever made her feel quite so warm.

"Since we had to reschedule our session today," he said, "are you going to make that up to me?"

Her gaze dropped to his knee. "You up for a walk tomorrow?"

"How far?" Hope made his voice jump half an octave.

"Maybe a quarter mile." Her grin broke into a full-on smile. "With a walker."

His head whipped from side to side to make sure that no one else had heard what she'd said. And he dropped his voice until it was almost inaudible. "Are you kidding me? I'm not going to use…one of those things."

"Literally. You're my worst patient. Worse than any doctor I've ever worked with."

Actually, he was doing remarkably well. Once he'd figured out that he could trust his knee not to buckle, he'd walked several lengths of the room without crutches or handrails at their last appointment. In fact, he'd wanted to keep going.

Stopping him from pushing too hard was going to be her most difficult job.

He rolled his eyes and finally nodded. "Fine."

With a pat on his shoulder, she whispered, "It'll be our secret. I won't let anyone see you with it."

The planes of his face seemed to soften, his eyes filling with concern. "Are you doing okay?"

"Of course."

"I mean, have you had any more trouble? Have you seen Gary or Camilla tonight?"

Shivers gripped her entire body, but she shook her head. "Maybe they won't show."

"Maybe." He didn't believe it, either.

"Dunham!" They both jerked in the direction of the loud voice calling his name. "Where you been hiding?"

Luke's gaze jumped from Mandy to Will Gumble to the family approaching the booth, tickets in hand. Will charged toward them, the grin on his tan face stretching to its limit.

"I'm going to say hi." He squeezed Mandy's hand. "But I'll be here all night. And I'll keep my eyes open."

She nodded as he ambled toward his friend, who threw his arms around Luke like a long-lost brother. Their words were garbled by the sea of other voices, but the tone of pure joy couldn't be missed even over the crowd.

The family of four finally reached her, shoving tickets in her direction and cheering as they tossed the plastic discs into the booth. Too many smiles to count, Mandy tried hard to join in their laughter.

But a niggling worry at the back of her mind kept her eyes darting across the crowd, always on the lookout. Would Gary make good on his threat to show up? And if he was here, would Camilla be far behind?

If the other woman did show up, maybe she'd stick around long enough for the cops to question her. Or maybe just long enough to find her mark.

"We haven't seen you around much since we got back."

Luke nodded. Will was right. He hadn't ventured much farther from his parents' place than Mandy's office. "I'm not so good at pool on these things." He tapped the rubber foot of his crutches and tried to follow it with a sardonic grin.

Will's dark eyes filled with pity. "Man, I'm sorry. I know this is tough."

Luke bit back the urge to say that he had no idea what it was like to lose his job, his future, his girl on some foreign street with a name he couldn't even pronounce.

But Will was still his best friend. The guy who'd made sure he made it through BUD/S and who had shoved him on a chopper and gotten him out of Dodge on the worst day of his life.

"I'm doing okay." And as Luke said the words, he realized that he meant them. And it was almost entirely due to the woman laughing with a family at the ring toss. He couldn't take his eyes off Mandy's face. She tossed her hair over her shoulder, the long waves shimmering in the light, like the sea beneath the moon. Her eyes danced, but the joy there was restrained at best.

He'd never met anyone quite like her. How could she be so graceful under fire? Gary or Camilla could be hiding in any number of dark corners, but Mandy still did whatever she could to make a child's night.

His ex, Bianca, had been pretty much the opposite.

He hadn't seen it at first. Young and blinded by outward beauty, he was all in before Bianca could snap her fingers. She'd been the reigning Miss Balboa County when they'd met. He'd just received his trident pin. She'd liked that he was a SEAL. He'd liked that she liked him.

It was easy to let himself off the hook for his own stupidity, but he should have known that she wasn't for him. She'd claimed to share his faith but always had an excuse for skipping Sunday-morning services. She'd promised to write him during his tours. She rarely had.

But she'd been intoxicating. And when he'd been near her, he couldn't help but be swept up in the party that was Bianca's life.

And then his knee had been ripped to shreds.

Bianca hadn't wasted any time calling to tell him it was over. "You're not a SEAL anymore. And I need more than a retired medic. I'm sorry, Luke."

He still felt the words, as surprising as the bomb that had killed his career.

But not nearly as strong.

Honestly, losing Bianca had been the easiest thing he'd faced at Walter Reed.

And she hadn't been cold or heartless. Just realistic about her own expectations for their life together—or rather, her life alone.

The truth was she did deserve more than a SEAL without a mission, without a future.

Mandy did, too.

When had he begun thinking of Mandy in terms of a future?

It didn't matter. Mandy was driven yet kind. Poised but

sometimes self-deprecating. And he wasn't the one for her. He couldn't be as long as his future remained so uncertain.

But for this minute he could keep her safe. And when this operation was over, he'd wish her well and walk away.

At least he could enjoy her smile for a little while longer.

Except just as she looked at him and he started to return her grin, her face turned stricken.

His gaze swept the crowd, but he didn't have to look far. Just a couple yards from her booth, Gary stood with his arms crossed and a knowing smirk in place. As the family left her side, Gary swayed toward Mandy, whose eyes grew large.

His movements were loose, almost too casual. And the red of his nose and cheeks boasted that he'd indulged in more than a bit of liquid courage.

Without a word to Will, Luke barreled through the crowd. He grimaced as he jarred his injured knee but kept going. Getting to Mandy was the important thing.

"You look amazing tonight," Gary slurred as he stepped into Mandy's personal space, forcing her to back up. She bumped into a tent pole behind her.

"Why are you here?" Her voice was firm but quiet, and Luke almost missed her next words. "I want you to leave."

He held up his hands as if to ward off an attack. "Hey, I paid money to be here, same as everyone else. I just wanted to come over and say—"

Luke clamped a hand on his shoulder, and Gary's words died, his mouth flapping like a fish. "She said she wants you to go."

Gary's fish face turned into a snarl as he turned back to Mandy. "Who does this guy think he is?"

Mandy's mouth opened once, then snapped closed. Her eyes lit with a fire that went beyond fear. But when she found her words, they were low and serious. "He's a friend. He's welcome here. You're not."

Apparently that response didn't settle well with Gary, who spun on Luke. "We have a history you know nothing about, so do yourself a favor and get lost." Then the guy had the gall to poke Luke in the chest.

Luke jerked away from the unexpected contact, then looked down at the spot where he'd been jabbed. "Seriously, man?"

Mandy looked as if she was going to be sick, but she mouthed an *I'm sorry* in Luke's direction.

Gary had no such courtesy. He just stared up at Luke, eyes filled with hate and arrogance and breath reeking of liquor. Luke had at least four inches and as many years of specialized hand-to-hand combat training on the guy. Clearly Gary had underestimated a man on crutches.

Bad idea.

Luke leaned in, a smirk slipping into place. "Trust me when I tell you, you should walk away. Right now. This—" Luke flicked his finger back and forth between them before resting it again on the handle of his crutch "—won't end well for you."

"Oh, really?" Gary pushed up his shirtsleeves, showing off a pair of tough-guy tattoos. In Luke's experience, guys with tats like that were trying too hard to prove something. "You're going to make me leave? You and what army?"

Who even said something like that? This guy was a real piece of work, and Luke had the urge to show him that he didn't need an army. Or even a wingman.

But before he could say the words on the tip of his tongue, the sound of three bodies jockeying for prime position around them interrupted him. Luke glanced over to see Will off to the right, his arms crossed and a relaxed expression on his face. Zig was on the left, running a hand over his bald head and giving Mandy an easy smile. Jordan, the biggest guy there, cocked his head and raised his eyebrows.

None of them said a thing as Gary held up his hands in surrender, his bravado withering. "Hey, man, we were just talking."

No army required. A SEAL team would do the job.

Just as Gary turned to leave, Mandy grabbed for the sleeve of his jacket. "Where's Camilla?"

That knowing grin fell back into place, in spite of her guards. "I don't have any idea." Then he jerked his arm out of Mandy's grasp and disappeared into the crowd.

It was a lie. One that could cost Mandy her life.

"You good, Cubby?"

Luke rolled his eyes at Zig, but the older SEAL wasn't likely to lay off the harassment with a pretty girl around. He never did. "We're good." The others tipped their heads and slipped away like steam evaporating.

"What did I ever see in him?" Mandy seemed to be asking herself, so Luke did the only thing he knew to do to offer a measure of comfort. He slipped his hand into hers and squeezed. She squeezed back, and sparks shot up his arm. After a long moment, she looked up, all brown eyes and fair freckles. "Thank you."

"We're in this together, remember?"

"You say that enough that I couldn't forget if I wanted to." Her lips held a funny little frown, but her tone of voice rang with humor.

"Just making sure."

The rest of the night went off without a hitch, without any sign of Camilla. And as the clock struck ten, dads picked up their sleepy children, and moms pushed strollers toward the parking lot. A few minutes later, Mandy made her exit, saying goodbye to the event's hostess and several other friends.

Luke watched her walk out with Matt and Ashley and their two little ones. He offered a small wave when she turned and caught his eye. She nodded back, then cupped her bare elbows against a stiff breeze.

Hadn't she had a sweater before? He was almost sure.

Hustling toward the ring-toss booth, he spotted the deep green pullover that she'd worn earlier. She must have forgotten it.

He picked it up, running the smooth and supple fabric over his hands. A thread caught on one of his calluses, and he carefully released it before tucking the light jacket over his shoulder. He could give it back to her the next day when they met up for his walk.

He moved toward his car as a workman began tearing down the booths, packing up each tent and the contents from within. Most of the SEALs and all of the families had cleared out, and the parking lot was nearly deserted except for the trucks and trailers that would haul away the evening's entertainment.

Tossing Mandy's sweater onto his car's passenger seat, he stowed his crutches in the back, angled himself into place behind the wheel and adjusted his leg.

His gaze dropped onto the sweater. Again.

Tomorrow. He'd see her then. In fact, first thing in the morning.

The sweater could wait.

But he wasn't sure he could.

Pulling onto the road, his car seemed to make the decision for him. It zipped toward Mandy's house as he relived her every expression from that night. Every laugh. Even the fear-filled gasp when Gary had shown up.

A vise at his temples squeezed, and he rubbed a fist across his forehead.

The guy made Luke want to punch a wall and find a safe house where Mandy could never be found. But was he really the one trying to kill her? Gary sure knew more about Camilla than he was revealing, but what kind of intel did he have?

The cops, Mandy, even Luke, were all hanging their hopes on the idea that Camilla was behind everything.

Because if she wasn't after Mandy, then they were at square one.

Suddenly the screen on his phone lit up, and he hit the hands-free button. "This is Dunham."

"Luke?" Her voice was reedy, but he'd know it anywhere.

"Mandy, what's wrong?"

"No-thing." But the dismissive remark didn't cover the hitch or the long pause that grabbed his heart with its talons. "I'm— The cops are already on their way."

The air in his car vanished. But he didn't need to breathe. He just needed to get there. Get to Mandy. Only two stoplights to go.

He pressed his foot against the accelerator, sailing through a yellow light and screeching into a turn on two wheels. "I'll be there in ninety seconds. Are you safe?"

"Yes. No. I—I don't know."

Icicles of fear stabbed through him as he skidded around the last turn, every worst scenario playing through his mind.

"I'm here." He grabbed his phone, snagged one of his crutches and flung open his door as Mandy ran out of her house. They met in the middle of the lawn. He held out his free arm, and she threw hers around his middle, her face burying into his chest.

"She was in there." Mandy's entire body trembled, each syllable taking every ounce of her strength. "She was in my house."

"How do you know?"

Eyes as wide as the Pacific lifted up to meet his gaze.

"She left me a note."

Everything inside him screamed not to ask. But he had to. He had to know. "What did it say?"

"She won't miss again."

SEVEN

Luke sighed into her hair, and Mandy let herself fall fully into his embrace. The arm not hanging on to his single crutch wrapped around her waist. And the rapid tempo of his heartbeat below her ear matched her own.

"Is she still in there?"

The ground seemed to open up below her, and she clung to him to keep herself standing. "I don't know."

His head turned toward the open door, and she felt his entire body sway in that direction. He was going to go inside to check. But the very thought made her feel like a kite caught in a tornado.

"Please, don't go." Oh, how she hated the way her voice pitched to the storm raging inside. Clearing her throat, she tried again. "I mean, the police will be here in a minute." *And I don't want to be alone.*

She couldn't admit that aloud, but it didn't change the truth. She'd come to rely on Luke, to look forward to his appointments and his smiling face. And he'd been there for her. Every step of the way, insisting that they were a team, promising he wasn't going to leave her.

And, so far, he'd kept that promise.

But this reliance, this dependence on a patient made her uneasy. Still, she couldn't step away from his strength.

She didn't want to.

His arm tightened around her as he looked across the row of empty, square lawns. She followed the direction of his gaze and froze as an eerie shadow slinked across the grass three doors down. Her shoulders erupted in tingles, and she wrenched in the opposite direction. Someone was watching her. Watching them.

Down the street a trash can crashed to the ground, its metal lid clanging against a driveway. She nearly jumped onto Luke's back, hiding her face in his shirt and praying for some heaven-sent help.

"We're too exposed out here." He tugged on her arm and tucked her into his side, his gaze always sweeping, always prying into the darkness.

What did his trained eyes see? Could he spot the person threatening her life? Or the barrel of a gun pointed at them? Everything inside her turned to ice. When she finally forced a breath over tight lips, she was pretty sure she could make out the cloud it left. "Who's out there?"

With uneven steps, he moved them along the smooth stone walkway. "I'm not sure. But I don't think it's a friend."

Her mouth went dry, and she couldn't even swallow the lump at the back of her throat. She wasn't imagining this. The weight of someone watching her wasn't an illusion. It wasn't a prank or a joke.

All of this was real.

Oh, Lord. Let this end soon. I can't live like this. You've got to save me.

With one last glance down her street, Luke closed the door on the night. With a flip of the lock, they were secure.

But were they alone?

Mandy's pulse rate tripled at the thought of being locked inside with her visitor—with Camilla. But when she opened her mouth to speak, nothing came out.

Luke rubbed his hands up and down her arms, his gaze never straying from hers. "I'm going to look around." He tried for an encouraging smile, but it ended up more like a grimace.

She could muster only a quick shake of her head. He couldn't leave her. He just couldn't. She needed a minute to pull herself together. He couldn't go until she had a firm grip on reality. He'd promised.

"Want to come with?"

She nodded.

"Okay. I want you to stay right behind me."

Another nod.

He shook his head in response. "Not just at my side. I want you staring at the middle of my back and holding on to my waist." He moved her hand to his right side, patting it into place so she could feel the even rise and fall. His words were thick with intensity, but the rhythm of his breathing never wavered. Always even. Always controlled. Always confident. "No matter what you hear, don't let go, and don't try to look around me. Got it?"

If he was an anchor, she was the ocean in a storm, cresting and falling, swooping and crashing.

Using his single crutch to keep the weight off his injured knee, he took a slow step forward. Everything inside her jolted.

Dear God, don't let there be anyone in my house. Please. Please!

She managed to follow his lead with a clumsy step. When she grabbed his side to stabilize herself, she jerked away. She couldn't add more pull on his body. Not when he wasn't evenly balanced.

He glanced over his shoulder. "You okay?"

She nodded. "Did I hurt you?"

His eyebrows formed a loose V. "No." Then with a nod of his head, his features returned to normal, and he stepped into the hallway.

First the coat closet. The door creaked as he opened it,

and she hoped it wasn't a mess. Of course, it always was. There was no helping the piles of reusable shopping bags stacked on top of saved shoe boxes beside the broken vacuum. He swished his hand through the half dozen coats hanging there. Satisfied, he closed the door and walked to the kitchen.

He entered slowly, peeking around the corner. And when he was sure it was safe, he lifted one hand and made a quick motion for her to keep up, but the knot in her stomach pulled so tight that she could barely move.

"Are you all right?" he asked when she lagged behind as he limped past the dining table she'd rescued from a '50s-era diner.

"Yes. I think so." Her own throat tried to strangle the words as he systematically checked every cupboard and entrance.

When he pulled open the back door, a chill swept through the room, and Mandy stepped even closer to Luke's warmth. He smelled like the night air and a hint of the cotton candy that had been liberally passed around at the carnival.

After the kitchen was the spare bedroom. They moved on to her room, where she closed her eyes and prayed she hadn't left anything embarrassing lying around. Luke paused for a moment, but he didn't say anything. Then as he looked into her closet, the entire ceiling creaked.

"Is there anything up there? A second floor?"

She shook her head and the house moaned again. Eerie and low, it wrapped around them, stealing her nerve. She tugged on his shirt. "Let's go."

He patted her hand and then wrapped his arm around her waist to hold her close. "We don't know that it's any safer outside."

Why did he have to remind her?

She glanced at her bed and wished with all her might

that she could just crawl into it, pull the covers over her head and stay there until there wasn't someone out there trying to kill her.

The ceiling creaked again, and they both jerked their chins toward it. He whispered, "Do you have an attic or crawl space?"

Jaw clamped too tight to speak, she managed just a nod.

His gaze dropped to his knee brace, and he let out a low growl. "I can't make it up there." His words sounded as if they were laced with lemon juice.

Sweat covered her forehead. She swiped it off with the back of her hand and croaked out an offer. "I—I can look."

His eyebrow cocked so high it was almost humorous. "Or we can wait for the police."

She let out a rush of air, relief coursing through her. Right. The police. They were on their way.

Luke took her hand in his, pulling her back through the house, keeping his pace easy. "I don't think there's anyone up there." When he reached the front window, he spread the blinds with two fingers and peered into the inky night. "But we'll wait by the door, just in case."

"How do you know?"

His gaze shifted over her head toward the hallway attic entrance. "No footsteps."

Of course. She was wound so tight that she hadn't even thought about the noises that her old house so often made. "It does groan like that sometimes."

He leaned against the back of the sofa, rested his crutch at his side and stared straight into her eyes. His gaze searched deeper than the surface, deeper than she was comfortable, but there was no looking away. The planes of his face went taut, and a muscle in his jaw twitched. "I'll stay with you. When the cops get here."

"Thank you." Her voice suddenly sounded breathless and airy, and she didn't want to think about why.

"And you can't stay here by yourself. It's not safe."

She wanted to argue. He didn't have to tell her what to do. Except he was right.

She'd be a fool to stay at her house as long as Camilla's whereabouts were unknown.

He slipped both of his hands around hers, holding them loosely between them, and she looked down to the point where his left thumb made loose circles on the back of her right hand. "I can help you find a secure place to stay."

Could any man be so genuinely concerned for her well-being?

Suddenly the question popped out of her mouth. "What's in this for you?" She pulled one of her hands out of his and slapped it over her mouth.

"For me?" He chewed on the corner of his lip for a long moment, his eyes angled toward the ceiling. "Well, there's the exceptional company. And the dental plan."

She shoved his shoulder, and he barely moved. "Be serious."

"All right." With a slow brush of his thumb across her cheek, he leaned in a fraction of an inch. "Seriously. I think you're a pretty incredible woman. You don't deserve this. And you could use a hand." The tone of his voice dropped, so she lifted her gaze until she could watch his mouth form the words. "I've got some time on my hands and some skills that might be useful to you."

He wrapped an arm around her waist, tugging her closer and splitting the distance between them again. And again.

How she'd ended up so fully in his embrace, she didn't know. What she did know was she didn't want to be anywhere else.

Her head began to spin, the tumult in her stomach anything but the fear she'd felt since reading the note. Like butterflies playing baseball, her insides fluttered.

His fingers combed the hair over her ears, and he rubbed

a strand between his thumb and forefinger. She leaned into his touch, her skin tingling at the brief contact.

Slipping her hand up his arm, over his shoulder and into his loose curls, she gave him the same treatment. His eyes crinkled at the corners, even though the smile never reached his lips.

Oh, his lips. Suddenly she couldn't see anything but his perfectly shaped mouth. And she couldn't think of anything but how it would feel when he pressed them to hers. Her breath caught, but who needed oxygen when he was about to give her the kiss she hadn't even realized she wanted?

He dipped his head, but his eyes were still open, waiting, asking if this was all right.

It wasn't right.

But she didn't care.

Squeezing her eyes closed, she held her breath and waited for the sparks.

Suddenly the telltale sirens of a police car broke the spell.

Mandy pulled away, and Luke's hands dropped to the couch, leaving only cold where they'd been.

He shuffled across the carpet and opened the door before the officer could even knock.

Shaking the cobwebs from her mind, Mandy plastered a half smile into place and stumbled over to meet the grizzled officer. His white hair stood on end, but the concern in his deep brown eyes was genuine. "Ma'am, I'm Officer Wilson." He shook her hand. "We had a report of a B and E. Are you the home owner?"

"I am."

Wilson's eyes shifted toward Luke, and he gave him a quick once-over, all the while sucking on his front tooth. He didn't speak, but his question was loud and clear.

Mandy jumped in to answer it. "This is my friend Luke."

Wilson gave Luke another glance, then turned back to Mandy. "Can you show me where the intruder gained access and what was taken?"

"Oh, there wasn't anything taken, and I don't know how she got in."

The wrinkles around his mouth deepened as he pursed his lips. "What do you mean?"

"The door was locked and the alarm activated when I got here."

His mouth took on a full frown, and his eyes, which had been filled with compassion, turned uncertain.

She glanced at Luke, expecting him to step in, but he kept his distance, prodding her on with an encouraging nod from the opposite side of her end table.

Lifting her chin, Mandy said, "Someone's been stalking me, and tonight she left me a note. Inside my house."

That perked up the officer. "Is there an open case file?"

"I've been reporting the incidents to Detective Fletcher."

Officer Wilson pulled out a notepad and jotted down the name. "I don't know him. Do you have his number?"

Mandy stooped to pick up her purse where she'd dropped it on the floor when she'd realized that the light she'd left on that afternoon had been turned off. In that moment, she'd known someone else had been inside her home. Digging through her wallet, she pulled out the detective's card and handed it to the uniformed officer.

He scribbled down the number as the radio at his shoulder squawked. He scrambled to turn it down before passing the card back to her.

"Do you mind if my partner and I look around for a point of entry?"

She hadn't even noticed the rail of a man standing in Wilson's shadow. But at Wilson's words, he leaned to the side, his hand snaking around his partner's arm to shake her hand. "Officer Gomez." He didn't say anything else, promptly disappearing into the shadows once again.

Mandy swept a hand, indicating her home. "Please." They were halfway to the kitchen when she called after them, "Would you mind checking the attic, too? We couldn't get up there."

Gomez looked over his shoulder, confusion marring his features until Luke tapped on his knee brace. With a shrug, the cop pulled on the release to the attic, climbed the ladder and shined his flashlight into the darkness above.

"Nothing."

And that was what they found in the rest of the house, too. After a thorough inspection of windows and doors, both interior and exterior, the officers met Mandy and Luke in the living room. Stymied, they looked at each other and finally shrugged.

"There's no sign of any forced entry," Officer Wilson finally conceded. "The locks are all intact. The windows are whole and latched. No sign that anything has been jimmied or broken."

He paused for a long moment, and Mandy didn't dare breathe. Maybe it was because she knew what was coming next. Or maybe it was because she hoped she was wrong.

"Whoever was in here had a key, knew your alarm code and covered their tracks."

Her stomach dropped to her feet, and she reached out for the back of the couch to steady herself. Instead she found Luke's hand, firm and callused and exactly what she needed.

He squeezed her fingers, and she could breathe again.

"Could we see the note that was left?" Mild-mannered Gomez looked genuinely upset that they hadn't found anything substantial, and he seemed unwilling to leave without trying again.

With her free hand, she pointed at the end table, where a simple white sheet of paper was tented by the base of the lamp. The outside was blank, so Gomez—still wearing his gloves—picked it up by the corner and read the words that had been printed there.

Mandy didn't need to see it again. The words had been seared on her mind's eye.

You may have gotten lucky before, but I won't miss again.

Wilson read over his partner's shoulder and, without looking up, asked, "How do you know it was a woman?"

Mandy opened her mouth, then snapped it closed. She looked to Luke, whose forehead had wrinkled as though he was deep in thought.

She'd been assuming it was Camilla. Ever since Gary had showed back up in her life. And maybe it was her.

But what if it was someone else entirely? Someone who knew where she worked, where she lived and what her schedule was.

Someone who had been studying her for a long time.

EIGHT

The next day brought a chill in the air, and Luke inhaled the sweet scent of the ocean as he stepped out of his car at the address Mandy had given him at the carnival the night before. She had parked two spots down, where she leaned against the hood of her rental, her arms crossed over a pink T-shirt as bright as the bags beneath her eyes were dark.

"Good morning," she said, a yawn cracking her jaw. "You ready to go for a walk?"

He glanced toward the red track that encircled a lush football field. Its white lane lines had been freshly painted, and it looked as if it belonged to wealthy college athletes rather than the high school students he knew used it during the week.

"I suppose so." He glanced down, watching as his foot pressed against the black asphalt and fire exploded in his knee. Forcing his face to remain unaffected, he took another step. He couldn't stop the whoosh of air that escaped on a wheeze. "Wouldn't a swim be better than a walk today?"

She unfolded her arms and pressed her hands to her hips. "Are you trying to kill me?" Her face twisted more with each word. "Or just your chances for a full recovery?"

He laughed out loud at her overly animated facial expression, her affront clearly not fully realized.

"I don't swim."

"What?" He took another step without thinking and nearly buckled beneath the agony. He grabbed for his car door and hugged it under an arm until the flames in his leg were only a flicker. "You're kidding, right?"

"No." She locked her car with two staccato honks and nodded toward the track. "Ready?"

He glanced at the backseat, contemplating pulling out his crutches. He'd hoped that keeping a crutch at his side the night before would spare him this kind of pain. But his knee seemed to have a different opinion. Apparently he'd pushed a little too hard.

Clearly she could read his mind. Or more likely his hesitant movements. "Are you going to get your crutches?"

"I thought you were going to bring me a walker."

"I didn't have one tall enough for you. Besides, I'm not quite that cruel." Her lips pursed as if she was holding back a chuckle, and he forced aside the thought of just how close he'd come to kissing her. He'd been half an inch away—maybe less.

Oh, man. It would have been absurdly stupid. But that didn't mean he didn't want another chance.

Stop it. Don't think about that, Dunham.

It wasn't smart. It wasn't safe.

He yanked the back door open, pulled out the crutches and slammed it shut, forcing himself to think about what lay ahead. This walk and the next one. And the next. This was going to get him back on the teams.

Eventually.

Maybe.

"How's your knee feeling this morning?" Mandy took off through the gate and onto the track, and he had to hustle to catch up with her.

"Fine."

"You going to tell me the truth?"

He caught a quick glance of her face, out of the corner of his eye, as he finally settled into a rhythm. She hadn't looked his direction or even slowed her pace, but there was no doubt in her tone, almost as if she could feel the stress of his muscles in her own.

"How'd you know?"

"You only used one of your crutches last night and took a lot of steps on your leg." Now she risked a glance in his direction, her eyes filled with knowing and compassion. "No one can jump in that fast without feeling the pain."

"Why didn't you tell me to use them both?"

"I'm not your momma."

He snorted at her immediate retort, but she wasn't done.

"We've been over what a reinjury to your knee would cost you."

A certain end to his career.

"I'll do everything I can to help you get back in fighting shape, but you have to do your part, too."

He knew it. He'd always known it. A return to active duty was almost entirely up to him. With a couple ifs.

If he did his therapy.

If he could be patient.

If his knee cooperated.

That last one was the crux of the whole thing. And the only one entirely out of his control.

He didn't want to think about what he'd do if his body let him down. He couldn't and keep his sanity.

And his recovery hadn't crossed his mind even once the night before. Not since the moment he heard her strained voice over the phone. He'd known nothing but getting to her side and keeping her safe.

He hadn't thought about it until he woke up sore and aching. But didn't want to talk about his pain.

Luke grasped at the first thing that popped into his mind

as they rounded the end of the track, halfway through their first lap. "So, you don't swim? At all?"

"No. I don't like the feeling of being out of control, and I'm afraid of being sucked into a riptide." She was so matter-of-fact about the whole thing that he thought she might be teasing him again. But there was no break in her smile or twinkle in her eye. There were only measured, even steps and unblinking eyes.

"But a pool doesn't have a riptide."

"I know." No argument. No excuses. Only the certainty that she knew herself and knew what she liked.

He couldn't hold back a smile. Good grief, that utter confidence was appealing. Along with her wry wit and eyes the color of dark chocolate. They were so expressive. So kind. So beautiful.

Get yourself together, Dunham.

She pressed a hand to her mouth as another yawn gripped her.

"How'd you sleep last night?"

She glanced toward the sky, seeming to follow the only cloud dancing across a canvas of blue. "Fine. I mean, it wasn't ideal, but I'm fine."

Fine. There had never been a more benign word that could cover such a multitude of emotions.

In the tension of her neck below a bouncing ponytail and in the tightness around her mouth, he could see that for the moment *fine* covered for fear.

"Did you get any sleep at all?"

She shrugged, her tennis shoes slapping against the Tartan track. "A little bit."

"Was there a problem at the hotel?"

Her forehead wrinkled, and she waved her hands in front of her. "No. It was fine."

There was that word again.

After the police had left the night before, he'd offered

the guest room at his parents' home, but she'd insisted on finding a hotel to stay in until whoever was after her was arrested. And a hotel was as secure as any home would be. But she was still alone.

She didn't need to be on her own, but no matter how many times he told her he would stay by her side, she didn't seem to believe it. Or she didn't know how to accept it. Even after he'd followed her to a hotel and made sure she was checked in, he'd seen the emotion in her eyes. Why did she force herself to face this threat on her own, even when she didn't want to?

Despite physical exhaustion, he'd tossed and turned the entire night, wondering if she was all right, wondering if he should have stayed in the parking lot until she was up. What if the fire alarm had gone off or there'd been an emergency?

And was it possible Officer Wilson had been right and Camilla wasn't the one after her? Had they made a potentially deadly assumption?

"Were you awake thinking about who else might be after you?"

Mandy slammed to a stop. "How'd you know?"

He smiled as she asked the same question he'd posed just minutes, just steps, before. "You have your expertise. I have mine."

Her eyes narrowed. "I thought yours was navy medicine."

"I didn't mean my job." He adjusted his crutches so they'd quit rubbing on a sore spot under his arm. "I know people in jeopardy. I know what they think about, how they react."

Two little lines formed between her eyebrows, and her lips grew tight. "And how do people in danger act?"

Talk about a loaded question. She had no idea how many memories that seemingly simple question conjured. Locked trunks. The unending shriek of an AK-47. A throat so dry he couldn't swallow and nothing but desert for miles around.

His firsthand experience had taught him that when someone's life was on the line, that person thought about only one thing: survival.

Mandy was looking for a shelter. And now the cops the night before had planted a seed that neither of them could ignore. If Camilla wasn't after Mandy, they had to figure out who was.

He could feel her gaze heavy on his back. Instead of turning toward her, he lifted his face to the breeze, breathing in the heady aroma of fresh air and freedom.

This wasn't the time to tell her about the danger he'd survived, even as a child. This was the time to find out who else they should be looking into. They didn't have any time to lose.

But maybe if he wanted her to trust him, he was going to have to give her something to show he trusted her. Just a little bit.

"One time when I was in Ly—in the Middle East, I was out on patrol with some marines." He stopped walking, as Mandy was still standing ten yards behind him and stubbornly refusing to move. But he didn't turn toward her. Keeping his voice just loud enough, he said, "One of the guys took a stray bullet to the arm, near a café. It wasn't life threatening, but I was the only corpsman for miles." Suddenly the memories flooded through him, and his throat closed.

This had been a terrible idea. He wasn't ready to talk about this. He wasn't ready to share.

He risked a glance in Mandy's direction, and her throat was tense. Her arms hung loosely at her sides, but her hands were balled into fists. "What happened?"

It would have been so easy to say that he'd patched the guy up and they'd gone back to the base. Man, he wished he could say that. He didn't want to relive that street or remember the rancid odor of burned flesh.

But he'd gotten himself into this. He'd started the story, and he was either going to have to finish it or lie for all he was worth. The second wasn't really an option, so he took a deep breath and rubbed a hand over his face.

"It was a busy area, packed with people who were almost entirely unfazed by the sound of gunfire, so I jogged across the street to patch up the guy. I was weaving in and out of the crowd, and I caught a glimpse of this man. He was a little bit behind me, and his eyes were jumpy, shifting back and forth. His arms were skinny, but his middle bulged beneath his coat."

Luke bit his tongue as a surge of chills raced down his spine, just as they had all those weeks ago. He'd felt the man's gaze, known that there was danger.

But he'd been unable to respond fast enough.

Mandy ran to his side, reaching out to him, then pulling her hand back. Opening her mouth to speak, then closing it. Those big brown eyes swam in pools of tears. She knew exactly where this story was heading.

As much as he wanted to stop it, to let her fill in the rest of the story with her own imagination, he couldn't. Now the words wouldn't stop.

"I knew that he was a threat. I *knew* that I had to do something." Her hand twined into his. "I lunged for him, just as he opened his jacket, and the entire world exploded. Everyone was screaming. The air was filled with debris. I was flat on my back, just staring at the gray haze hovering over the road.

"But mostly there was screaming. The marines started yelling for the medic, each call louder and louder. They were calling for *me*. And I could hear them, but I couldn't do a thing about it. I could only try to assess my own losses and pray that God would either take me right then or send another medic."

"Did He? Send another medic, I mean?" Her grip on his hand turned severe, almost as if she didn't realize that he had survived and was standing beside her now.

Luke chuckled at the question. "Not exactly. He sent me Corporal Jonathan Dunbar, a marine the size of a house, who picked me up like a sack of potatoes, threw me in the back of a Humvee and got us back to the base."

When the story was over, he let out a sigh of relief. He'd survived. He'd been back on that Lybanian street for a moment, but somehow Mandy had been with him, holding his hand through the whole thing. Bianca hadn't known how to walk an uncertain path, but Mandy not only knew how to, she gave him strength for those moments he wasn't so sure he could.

Incredible.

"I'm glad that God didn't take you then."

He jumped at Mandy's words, then let out a belly laugh. "Me, too."

She ducked her head, and a faint blush crept up her neck. "You know what I mean."

"I do." He gave her hand a reassuring squeeze. "I've been where you are. You can tell me why you couldn't sleep last night. Maybe it'll help."

She tried to pull her hand out of his, but he didn't let her retreat into herself. Instead he set down his crutches and took a slow step, coaxing her along with him. Her gaze stayed somewhere close to her feet, and her voice was quiet when she first spoke. "What if it's not Camilla?"

Mandy caught Luke's brief nod out of the corner of her eye, afraid of the answer to her own question. Without Camilla, her only suspect was Gary himself. But Gary hadn't been a part of her life for years. Why would he choose to make her life miserable now when he'd already done it once? It just didn't add up. "She'd have to know everything about me to do what she's been doing, to know how to get into my house. And some of these things have been going on a long time. Gary and Camilla only split recently."

Luke made a noise of assent but didn't interrupt her processing.

"But why? Who has reason to want to see me gone? Camilla at least has a reason to hate me."

"She does?"

Her stomach flipped at his question, and not for the first time, she fought the urge to tell him the whole truth. But she couldn't. She wouldn't. So she just shook her head. "Who else could it be?"

He stared across the field, to the gate where they'd started almost two laps before, but he seemed to see something else. "You said, when we first met, that some of your cases don't end up like you'd like."

She tripped on the toe of her tennis shoe and nearly swallowed her tongue. Only his hand on her elbow kept her upright as she shook her head violently at the very thought. "You think it's an unhappy patient?" It couldn't be. That was absolutely ludicrous. Wasn't it?

"Maybe."

"No." She yanked her arm loose. "There's no way. I don't make any promises to my patients. You know that. I can't control the human body."

"Are there any cases that make you cringe when you think about them?"

On cue, her stomach gave a violent twist and sickening lurch. "You mean other than Gary?"

He nodded but didn't even grin at her attempt at levity. "Yes."

"Like which ones?"

He hadn't wanted to talk about that suicide bomber.

She'd seen it written all over his face. Now she knew exactly how he felt. It was like being sick to her stomach and unable to lie down, this feeling of knowing that she had to tell him but hating to dredge up the memories.

The past had a power all its own, and right that minute, she hated every bitter moment it held.

Still, it was the lesser of two evils. Pouring salt onto mostly healed wounds was better than opening new ones. And if they didn't stop whoever was after her, the new wounds were liable to be fatal.

Squeezing her hands into a fist, she steeled herself to tiptoe down memory lane. "I was fresh out of my doctorate program, top of my class and certain that all of my patients were headed for a full recovery. I was working under another PT, who warned me that one of my knee patients was pushing too hard. But I was sure he could take it. He couldn't. He ended up tearing his ACL only weeks after his first surgery."

Luke grimaced. "So that's why you're always harping on me to be patient."

"No. I harp on you to be patient because it's what's best for your recovery."

"Fair enough," he said. Making a slow turn, he returned to the spot where he'd dropped his crutches on the track and stooped to pick them up. "I guess I'll call that a day."

She smiled and tipped her chin toward the parking lot. As they ambled in that direction, he prompted her for more cases.

"There was a young girl who had been born without either leg, and her parents wanted me to help her get prosthetics, but they didn't have insurance." She pulled open the chain-link gate and held it as he swung through. "I gave them the name of several agencies that might be able to help them, but there was nothing I personally could do.

The dad flew off the handle, yelling at me. But that was years ago. Why would they wait so long?"

"I don't know."

When they reached her car, she paused, a tiny memory trying to push its way to the top of her mind. "There was someone else. But not a patient. Not officially anyway."

He nodded his encouragement, and she closed her eyes, trying to see the face that was taking shape. "She had been in a car accident, paralyzed from the waist down. She came in for a consultation several years ago, and she was in bad shape physically. But more so, she wasn't mentally ready to face the very real possibility that she'd never walk again."

Luke's eyes turned soft, knowing. "What happened to her?"

"I told her I couldn't work with her until she saw a counselor and worked through her issues." A strange emotion, like remorse combined with pity, rolled through her, surprisingly strong, even after so many years.

"And?"

"I heard a few months later—" her voice broke, and she cleared her throat "—that she committed suicide."

Luke pulled her into a hug, his arms as warm as the sunshine and infinitely more compassionate. "I'm so sorry."

"I haven't thought about her in well over a year. I don't know what made me think of her now."

"Maybe that the loss of a daughter might spur parents to target someone they blamed."

Again that sick twist deep inside. He was right. "It's been so long. Why would they carry a grudge that long? Or blame me?"

"People in pain look for someone to blame. And maybe they latched on to you."

"But maybe it's not them." Mandy didn't even sound convinced to her own ears. And she could tell that Luke was just humoring her when he shrugged a hesitant agreement. "I should call Detective Fletcher and tell him about these cases anyway, shouldn't I?"

"I would."

Only one problem. She couldn't remember any of their names. "I have to go to the office first."

He seemed to understand, swinging toward his car.

"So, I'll see you on Monday at your appointment?"

He laughed. "I'll follow you to your office. I'll see you there in ten minutes."

True to his word, Luke stayed right behind her as she weaved through traffic. And when she pulled into the spot directly outside the side door, he parked his car right next to hers, joining a third vehicle. All of the medical offices in the complex were closed for the weekend, but an enormous black SUV was parked right in front of her building.

From the driver's seat of his car, Luke caught her eye and nodded in the direction of the monstrosity.

She shook her head. She had no idea who it could be.

They both looked back at it just as the driver's door swung open and Gary slithered from behind the wheel. He straightened the cuffs of his long-sleeved, button-up shirt and ran his hand over the fabric to release any wrinkles before sauntering in their direction.

This guy didn't know when to give up.

He was plenty arrogant to believe that she didn't mean it when she told him she didn't want to see him again. But was he duplicitous enough to play at wooing her while actually trying to kill her?

Her blood began to pound in her ears, pressure building at her temples. Her breaths came out in short gasps, and she smacked a hand against her steering wheel, accidentally hitting the horn and making all three people in the parking lot jump.

Shooting out of her car, she slammed the door closed.

Luke's door followed in quick succession, his presence silent but supportive.

Gary hurried to her, ignoring Luke, and reached for both of her hands. "When you weren't at home, I knew I'd find you here."

She pulled her hands out of his reach but took a wide stance and glared at him with the full force of everything inside her. "I'm done with this."

"Please, baby. I miss you. Last night was a misunderstanding."

"Don't!" The scream was louder than she'd intended it, but it did the job of shocking him into silence. "I. Don't. Want. To. See. You. Again."

"You don't mean that."

What had she ever, ever seen in this jerk? He clearly didn't listen to her, and he sure as fire didn't care about her. "I promise you, I do. And if you show up again, I will get a restraining order against you."

The threat of legal action made his too-sharp chin twitch, and he patted his perfectly coiffed hair, as though he didn't know what to do with his hands.

In Gary's stunned silence, she risked a look in Luke's direction. He was all stone wall except for the sparkle in his eyes and the barely concealed grin tugging at his lips. *Good job.* He only mouthed the words, but they gave her the gumption to take two steps toward Gary.

"I'm not teasing or kidding around. I will send the cops after you."

Gary blinked three times in a row. His mouth remained blessedly closed.

"Now, tell me you understand what I'm saying."

"I'm not sure—"

"No. I want to hear you say you understand."

His forehead wrinkled and eyes narrowed to slits. "I won't be back."

"That's the point. But still not what I want to hear." Who was this woman making these demands and so absolutely sure of what she wanted and needed? Mandy didn't feel entirely like herself. Always with her patients, she was confident. But when it came to her personal life, Gary had made her doubt and second-guess nearly every step of it.

Until Luke had showed up. What was it about him that gave her the courage to say exactly what she needed to?

Gary's eyes lit with an inferno burning too hot. His nostrils flared, and his lips all but disappeared into a line. With another quick check of his appearance, smoothing his arm sleeves and making sure his shirt was tucked into his khakis, he spun on his heel and marched toward his car. With a thud, his door closed behind him, and he peeled out of the parking lot. He didn't even stop before pulling onto the street to the sound of several wailing horns.

When his car had disappeared, she turned to Luke, who was already at her side.

"Brilliant." His whisper danced over the top of her head as he slid his arms around her waist and invited her to snuggle into his warmth. After her confrontation with Gary, she should have pushed Luke away. Instead she sank into his embrace.

"Where'd you learn to be so tough?" he asked.

Tough? She felt more like a wounded duckling. Every inch of her trembled. If she was tough, she'd have done that when Gary first came into her life. If she was tough, she wouldn't be clinging to Luke just to stay on her feet.

Her hands were fisted into the front of his T-shirt, and she tried to let go, but it was going to take a little while to pry her fingers from their purchase.

"I just need a minute." The words were muffled against his shoulder, and she rocked her face against the soft knit fabric there, trying to force her legs to start working, trying to force herself to let go.

"Take your time." He drew an easy circle on her back with the palm of his hand, each pass soothing the knots there. "You were fantastic. I've never seen anyone stand their ground like you just did. I'm proud of you." He punctuated his words with a gentle brush of his lips against her temple, and everything inside her turned to Jell-O.

No. No. No.

She jumped away, praying her legs would hold her. Although she wobbled a bit, she stayed upright. Shoving her hands to her sides, she grabbed on to her exercise pants, twisting the stretchy fabric until her insides returned to rights.

That was how things had started with Gary. Gentle embraces. Almost kisses. Seemingly innocuous touches. And then one day, they suddenly weren't innocent.

No matter how gentle his touch or how much she liked it, Luke was still a patient.

"We shouldn't… We can't do that. Please."

Confusion, quickly followed by understanding, swept across his face.

"I need to go. I'm exhausted. I'm going to take the files back to my hotel." Her words rushed out, almost as one long word.

"All right."

He waited where he was as she ran inside, boxed up a section of former-patient files and carried them back to her car. "Gary's long gone. There's no reason for you to follow me back to the hotel."

He looked doubtful, but agreed after a long pause.

With a wave and a brief thank-you, she fled the scene and the emotions that Luke insisted on stirring inside her. Ones she hated. Ones she loved. Ones that made her hope for a future.

The stoplight right in front of her turned red, and she slammed on her brakes, pressing against the taut seat belt that rubbed where she still had bruises. With a groan, she tucked her hair behind her ears before rubbing the back of her neck. She needed some ibuprofen and a good night of sleep.

And something to make her dislike Luke. Something strong.

At least she had the first at her house. It would be only a quick detour to run by her place. And then she could pick up her favorite sweater and an extra pair of jeans, which she'd forgotten to pack in her rush the night before.

Somehow her cute little bungalow seemed like foreign territory in the setting sun. It had been taken by the enemy, and she sat in her car, parked on the street, working up the courage to run in.

Dear Lord, I'm scared. Keep me safe.

Whether she was afraid of another note promising an attempt on her life or that someone might be hiding inside, her heart thudded painfully, slowly. Whatever was inside, she could face it.

She'd have to eventually anyway, and this was as good of a time as any.

Racing across her lawn, she flung open the front door and swung it closed behind her. Immediately she slammed into a rotten-egg odor like she'd never smelled before. It permeated everything and clung to her clothes and her skin. Its rancid fingers sifted through her hair and wafted around her head.

She took three steps toward the alarm pad to push a button that would alert the authorities, but when she pressed her finger to the emergency alert, nothing happened. Its wires had been neatly trimmed. It was useless.

Mandy tried to catch her breath but only managed to cough and gag on the natural gas that filled her home and made her head spin. Tears rushed to her eyes, flowing freely down her face. She tripped on a rug, slamming into a wall and falling to her knees. Crawling toward the front door, she strained for the handle but couldn't reach the knob. A cloud settled over her mind, and she just wanted to sleep.

Luke's face flashed before her.

Fight.

He would tell her fight through this and get out. The tiniest spark could ignite this much natural gas. If the house blew, she was gone. Along with whatever evidence had been left behind.

Shoving her flat hands against the hardwood floor of the entry, she pushed herself up only to sink down again.

The gas made her feel as if she was seasick on a dinghy. With a heave and roll of her stomach, she lost her lunch on the floor.

She had to call for help.

But her fingers refused to do what she told them to. She watched them reach for the phone in her pocket, almost as if they belonged to someone else. She could only manage to call the last person who had called her.

Putting the phone by her ear, she listened to it ring once. Twice. Three times.

"Calling to schedule another walk already?"

Were those the last words she'd ever hear?

"'S Man-dy. At home. Gas."

And then she couldn't fight the haze any longer. It swallowed her completely, and everything around her faded to black.

NINE

"Mandy?"

Nothing. The line was live, but she didn't respond.

Luke tried again. Louder. "Mandy!"

There was only silence on the other end of the call. A fine sheen of sweat broke out across his forehead and down the back of his neck. She'd said there was gas, and she was in trouble. She needed him. ASAP.

He was nearly to his parents' place, so he whipped his car around, sailing up the on-ramp and north on I-5. For a Saturday night, traffic wasn't terrible, but everyone seemed to be content going the speed limit.

Luke was not.

As he swerved between cars, his heart thudded painfully, and his knuckles turned white around the steering wheel.

Heavenly Father, keep her safe. She matters to me.

He didn't want to think about how she'd come to be such an important part of his life in such a short time, but he couldn't deny the space that she now occupied in his heart and mind.

He had to get there in time. He just had to.

An ambulance heading south wailed down the left lane, its sirens crying out.

Sirens. He had to get her help. He couldn't save her

alone. Not if her house was filled with natural gas and possibly on the verge of exploding.

The emergency call button on his phone quickly connected him to a response team. "Nine-one-one, what is your emergency?" asked a female operator.

"A gas le-leak in Balboa Heights." Luke choked out the words. Getting them around his heart, which was firmly lodged in his throat, took two tries.

"What's the address?"

"I can't remember the house number." He'd been there twice, and he couldn't picture her address. Both times he'd just followed Mandy's directions. "But it's on Balboa Heights Lane. It's a little blue bungalow. The only one on the street."

The 911 operator typed something into the computer on her end, her fingers clacking against the keyboard. "Are you at the house?"

"No. I'm on my way there right now. But my friend is inside the house. I think she passed out before she could get out."

"How do you know?" The woman's voice switched from even professionalism to a hint of real concern.

Luke cut off another car to take the exit toward Mandy's subdivision, flying through a yellow light at the end of the ramp. "She called me. She was completely disoriented, and I don't think she can get out."

"Is there anyone else in the home?"

A scene from the search through Mandy's house the night before flashed across his mind. What if her stalker had come back? What if she was inside with Mandy? His vision narrowed as he skidded around another corner. "I'm not sure."

"I have the fire department and an ambulance en route. ETA three minutes." She paused for a long moment, and again, the clacking of keys filled the silence. "Sir, what's your name?"

What did it matter? Why was she wasting time when Mandy's life was on the line? Even though he knew she was only doing her job, he had to force himself to take a breath before responding. "Petty Officer Luke Dunham."

"Can you stay on the line with me, Petty Officer Dunham?"

As Luke pulled onto Mandy's street, he saw her car parked in front of her house. "No."

He didn't wait for an argument or goodbye before hanging up, parking on the far side of the street and flinging his car door open. Just as he did, sirens filled the evening, growing ever louder as they bore down on his location. Scrambling for his crutches from the backseat, he was just upright on them when a huge red fire engine swung onto the street. Standing in their headlights, he flagged them down and pointed to Mandy's home.

The beast of a truck rolled to a stop with a whine of its brakes, and men began jumping out of every available opening. Organized and orderly. They were much like the navy in that way.

A man, who took charge as if he was the captain, jumped out of the passenger seat, while his men began slipping their oxygen tanks over their shoulders.

"Did you call this in?" the captain asked.

"Yes, sir."

"You haven't been in the house, have you?" Piercing blue eyes swept over him.

"No." Only because the professionals had arrived before he could get across the street.

"Good." Those unflinching eyes locked in on him again. "Stay on the far side of the street until we give the all clear."

Luke nodded. There was no need to argue.

As three men with oxygen masks ventured toward the

front of house, another ran around the back. Most likely he was shutting off the gas main. On his return, he gave a thumbs-up, and the other three reached the front door.

Almost simultaneously, the ambulance appeared at the end of the street. It pulled into place opposite the fire truck, and a man and a woman in blue uniforms hopped out of the cab.

Someone's walkie-talkie squawked to life. "Woman down in the front entrance."

Luke didn't care if the fire captain had chained him to the other side of the street. Nothing was going to keep him from being at Mandy's side. His crutches clacked as he crossed the street as fast as he could make them go.

"Stay back," one firefighter said.

He locked gazes with the shorter man, channeling one of his SEAL instructors. "She's my responsibility."

The fireman saw something that made him nod and step back as one of his coworkers ran out of the house, carrying Mandy's limp form. Her arms hung at odd angles, her neck strained all the way back. Her skin was sallow, her lips nearly colorless.

Luke gasped at the change. In less than an hour, she'd turned into a shadow of her former self.

The paramedics had the gurney there in a moment, and Luke raced toward them, his heart beating twice as fast as his feet could move.

"Her pulse is weak, and her blood pressure is low." The woman pulled open Mandy's eyes and shined a flashlight into them. "Good pupil response. And there doesn't appear to be any head injury."

The other paramedic pressed a plastic mask to Mandy's face, lifting her head to secure it with an elastic band. A long tube ran from the front of the mask to an oxygen canister, and even in the yellow streetlights, he could see pink returning to her lips.

Slipping to her side, he grabbed her hand and laced his fingers with hers. When their palms pressed together, a shock ran up his arm.

"Mandy? Can you hear me?"

The female paramedic glanced from Luke to Mandy and back again. "Is she your girlfriend?"

Without even a thought, he opened his mouth and let his heart reply, "She's mine."

At his words, Mandy squeezed his hand, and her eyes flickered open. She took a deep breath that swelled her chest and gave her cheeks a hint of color.

Luke smiled like an idiot, his grin stretching his face so far that it nearly hurt. But he couldn't be bothered to notice something so trivial when the corners of Mandy's eyes crinkled with joy. A tiny spark there brought her back to him.

"Knew you'd—"

The paramedic touched her arm and shushed Mandy, who blinked several times before letting her eyes stay closed. The muscles in her face relaxed, and her breathing slowed as though she was finally finding restful sleep. He released his grip on her hand, but she held on so firmly that he couldn't let go.

Fine. He'd stay right where he was. No complaints.

Running a finger along her forehead, he smoothed her hair out of the way. It was like silk beneath his fingers, and he gave it another pass and a gentle caress. Mandy rewarded him with a shallow smile under her mask.

"We're going to take her to the hospital," the woman said.

Luke shook his head quickly. "She won't want to go."

Mandy gave a quick nod but stopped as her face twisted in pain. "I'm okay. I don't need to go…"

"Well, you can't stay here." The familiar voice was clear

and unyielding, like an elementary-school principal. Officer Wilson sauntered toward them.

This brought Mandy nearly upright, leaning on her elbows behind her. She pulled down the oxygen mask and let it hang around her neck.

"I was hoping I wouldn't be back out here again." Wilson seemed to think he'd made a joke, letting out a dry laugh. All the muscles in Luke's throat tightened in dread, and he couldn't respond.

Mandy, however, wasn't suffering the same paralysis. "What did you find?"

The cop held up an evidence bag, which contained a broken lightbulb. The glass casing had been shattered, but the filament and support wires were fully intact.

A collective gasp rose from their little group, and Mandy pushed herself farther up, bracing a hand behind her and holding her head with the other.

"The gas on the stove was turned all the way up, and the pilot light had been blown out. And this was in the hallway fixture." Wilson lowered the bag but kept his gaze fixed on Mandy. "Someone removed the outer globe and left this. If you'd flipped the hall light switch..."

Luke's body shivered, and Mandy's shoulders twitched. They both knew what would have happened. Mandy had managed to escape again. And whoever was after her wouldn't be happy that she'd dodged another figurative bullet. But there was no telling how long it would be before those bullets were real.

One look at her face, and Luke knew she was thinking the same thing. Her lips had regained their color but had nearly disappeared into a tight line, and the shimmering in her eyes wasn't from the flashing blue-and-red lights.

"Do you have somewhere safe to stay?" Wilson asked.

"I stayed at a hotel last night."

The officer shook his head as a paramedic pushed

Mandy's oxygen back into place. "Keep this on. It'll help your headache."

She nodded at the other woman before turning back to Wilson, who asked, "Are you alone?"

She offered a slow, affirming shrug.

"Is there someone who can stay with you? Someone else you can stay with? Especially tonight."

Mandy shook her head, her eyes as big and sad as the basset hound he'd had as a kid.

"She can stay with me." Luke was happy to be of service and for an excuse to keep her close. Even if his mission had just increased to a full-time job.

But would it be enough? If he never returned to the SEAL teams, would one-off jobs like this be enough? If God took away the thing he loved most on earth, being part of the elite brotherhood, would Luke be enough? These and a hundred other questions hooked on to the back of his mind.

He could only cling to the things he knew to be true. God loved him. Mandy's smile made him melt. And he was doing something he was good at: protecting the innocents and hunting down the tangos.

He risked a grin. "My parents have a guest apartment. She can stay with us until the threat is neutralized."

"No, I don't want to…" But her mask muffled her excuse, and Luke just shook his head until she finally nodded her acquiescence.

"Good. Now that that's settled—" Wilson pulled his notebook out of the back pocket of his uniform pants and flipped it open "—I talked to your Detective Fletcher today. He said there's still no news back from the CHP about the brakes on your car. And there's still no sign of Mrs. Heusen. She hasn't returned any of his calls. But I'll make sure he knows about what happened tonight."

Mandy looked at Luke, and he lifted his shoulders. More

and more he had doubts about Camilla's involvement. But if she wasn't targeting Mandy, why was she hiding from the police? If it wasn't Camilla, who was after Mandy? They needed to look at those files and start pulling some names from the cases she had mentioned. This vendetta was personal, and they were going to have to turn over every stone to figure out who was behind it.

The paramedic picked up her equipment bag. "If you're not going to the hospital, then we'll pack this up."

"Of course." Mandy hopped off the gurney and immediately looked as if she regretted her decision. Her legs buckled beneath her, and she fell into Luke's chest.

He wrapped an arm around her back and had to restrain himself from scooping her up into his arms. Once upon a time, he'd been able to comfort a woman that way. He could cradle her and protect her from the rest of the world.

But not right now.

He hated his leg for failing him. For bringing him to this very moment.

That idea slammed into him with the force of a train, and he dropped his arm. Was it possible that his injury—the one that could keep him from his greatest dream—had also brought Mandy into his life? What if he had never met her? What if he'd settled for a woman like Bianca without ever knowing an amazing woman like Mandy?

He shook his head. This wasn't the time or the place to think about those things.

But the rock in the pit of his stomach suggested that it might not be so easy to dismiss.

Right now, he needed to get Mandy to his parents' place so she could get some rest and they could give Detective Fletcher some names to look into.

The paramedics began tucking their tools of the trade back into large duffel bags and storing them inside the ambulance's bay. Luke bent as low as he could on his injured knee and looked right into Mandy's face. "Are you sure you're okay?"

She pressed a hand to her temple, wrapping her fingers over the top of her head as if it might fly off if she didn't hold it in place. "Just dizzy. My head is throbbing." She wrinkled her nose and pursed her lips. "And there's a serious mess to clean up inside my house when I can get back into it." She managed a shallow chuckle as her gaze dropped to the grass between the toes of her shoes. "Thank you for getting here as fast as you did. And calling the fire department. You saved my life. Again."

Usually when someone thanked him for a specific service, he played it off with a flippant joke. But the soft rise and fall of Mandy's shoulders gave him pause. She kept showing up in his thoughts about the future, and he wasn't nearly ready for her to walk out of his life.

Especially when he was in a position to make sure she stuck around.

"Anytime." He walked her toward his car. Settling her into the passenger seat, he closed the door and whispered, "Every time."

Mandy leaned her forehead against the cool glass of the car window. Its soothing temperature eased around her head, setting the uneven floor of her mind to rights.

This wasn't the first time she'd sat in this very seat and rested against this same window.

Luke was making a habit of rescuing her. And giving her confused looks every time she returned his comforting embrace but then pulled away when it turned into something more. Something deeper.

And now she was going to stay with him at his parents' place. Professional boundaries had flown out the window faster than she'd careened down that mountain a week before.

She had to put some kind of barrier in place. Her last attempt to keep her heart and actions in check. He deserved to know why she couldn't act on the feelings that refused to be subdued.

But when he tossed her box of files into the backseat, slid behind the wheel and held out his hand, she couldn't help but slip hers into it. "You'll be safe. Tomorrow we'll tackle the files. Tonight you can rest."

"Thank you."

The base of his neck, just above the collar of his US Navy sweatshirt, turned pink in the car's dim overhead light as he pulled away from the curb and around the last police car left on the block. But he didn't say a thing. Instead he gave her a slow, sad smile, almost as though he wished he could take her place in this whole mess.

Only, she didn't want him in danger. From a madman. Or even from her.

Letting go of his hand and clasping her own in her lap, she stared hard at her interlaced fingers, searching for the right words to explain her past and their present. Somehow they'd become intertwined—the before and the right now—and he deserved to know the truth about both.

With a silent prayer, she closed her eyes and opened her mouth. And the words began to tumble out. "I hadn't seen Gary for almost four years until he showed up at my office last week. He was a patient. And he was so charismatic."

She peeked at him as he turned the car toward the coast. His eyes never left the road, and a muscle in his jaw worked as if he were chewing on her words. But he didn't tell her to stop, so she kept going.

"One of my college professors had warned our class about the illusion of closeness that comes with the therapist-patient relationship. After spending multiple days a week together for months at a time, it's easy to feel close to someone. I get to share pain and triumph, joys and struggles with my patients. It's a special relationship, particularly in the medical field.

"But Gary surprised me. He pursued me in little ways. It started just two weeks into our sessions. I'd find notes, after he'd left, stuck on the outside of his patient chart. Then flowers delivered from a secret admirer."

"White roses." Luke's interruption was softly spoken but utterly certain.

"Yes. How did you know?"

He shrugged. "Tara might have mentioned they were your favorite."

Of course. "She's always up on the office gossip. No one knows more about what's going on than she does."

An expectant pause filled the car as lights on the side of the highway flew by, flickering in the car. Finally, he gave her a gentle nudge. "Go on."

But she didn't really want to, because she wasn't proud of the rest of her actions. She could have kept her distance. She should have shut him down.

So many should haves and could haves.

They all melded together in the haze that still encircled her mind, and she just waited for the words to start rolling out, praying that somehow Luke wouldn't find her as appalling as she found herself. "I was flattered by his kind words and thoughtful gifts, and I let my guard down. I told myself that he was just being friendly. And honestly, no one had ever pursued me with such focused attention."

Luke mumbled something under his breath that sounded as if he found that hard to believe, but she didn't stop to ask him to repeat it. This was hard enough without changing the subject. Twisting the hem of her shirt into a ball, she kept at it.

"And then one night we were alone in the office. Everyone else had gone home, even my office manager." She swallowed down the regret that burned the back of her throat, keeping her eyes fixed on the road. "I let him kiss me. Honestly I wanted it as much as he did. It was… Well, anyway, it went on for a while. But then I started hearing rumors. About another woman."

Risking a glance in his direction, she watched Luke's profile as she confessed. "I should have asked him about what I heard, but I didn't. Truthfully, I didn't want to know. It was just easier being in the dark, pretending that he loved me. After all, I had to see him twice a week at his appointments, and I wanted to keep seeing him on the other nights, too."

Luke's jaw flexed. Hard. "I'm sorry he cheated on you."

The words that had been so free-flowing suddenly caught on the back of her tongue, and she had to spit them out. "Not *on* me. *With* me."

The car veered into the left lane and then immediately back into its spot. The jolt rocked them both, but Luke got them on track, his jaw firm and unmoving.

"One of the assistant therapists at the office told me that Gary was engaged, but I couldn't stop seeing him. It was like being hypnotized. Everything I knew and believed didn't seem to matter because Gary had become my whole world. And I didn't want that to change."

Her stomach rolled at the memories. At the hurt that she'd caused. At the damage she'd done.

No, she hadn't been alone in her actions. Gary was equally to blame. He'd deceived her. He'd wooed her when he was already engaged to Camilla. He'd pursued her when he wasn't free to do so.

But she'd known better. She hadn't been walking with God at the time, but her heart recognized that what they were doing was wrong. And she'd had the chance—multiple chances—to find out the truth. She hadn't. Because it would have been hard. Because it would have meant giving up the person she thought loved her.

She knew the truth now. Gary had never loved anyone but himself. He'd never cared for anyone's feelings except his own.

Luke let out a long breath through tight lips, the only sound in the car for what felt like an eternity. "How did it end?"

"Camilla showed up at the office, waving around her two-carat engagement ring and screaming that I had to break things off with her fiancé. Then she threw a lamp on the floor and said that if I ever saw Gary again, she'd do the same to me. I begged her to forgive me, but she stormed away."

In the end, that encounter had been what prodded Mandy to go back to church. She'd been a woman without a compass, letting her feelings dictate her own right and wrong. And she'd wound up hating herself for it. Through Camilla's eyes, Mandy had seen the things she'd done for what they truly were—selfish and hurtful.

And she'd sworn to God that she'd never do something like that again.

"I haven't seen Camilla since, and I ended things with Gary that day."

Parking his car in front of a large two-story home with an excessively lush lawn, Luke paused. "Why tell me all of this now?"

Oh, Lord. The two-word prayer was the only thought she could muster for a moment. Had she completely and utterly misread the signals between them? Did he not feel the sparks when they touched? She could have explained Camilla's hate without all the detail. But she'd wanted him to understand why their relationship couldn't be anything more than physical therapist and patient.

"I'm sorry. I didn't mean… I just thought you should know since…"

The words died on her tongue as she hung her head,

her hair falling over her shoulders. Letting it serve as a curtain between them, she took a shaky breath and tried to keep the shame from her face.

The regrets still haunted her. It wasn't so much what she'd done as what she'd failed to do.

She hadn't known about Camilla when Gary first showed his interest. That wasn't her mistake to regret. But later, when the rumors were too loud to ignore, she'd done just that. She'd stuck her head in the sand because she didn't want to hear them.

Tears pooled in the corners of her eyes, and she swiped at them with her knuckles, wiping away the evidence on the leg of her workout pants.

How could she have been so careless, so thoughtless?

Even more than the sting of that truth was the censure she knew would come from Luke. A man of integrity wouldn't just overlook her sins. And she knew him to be just that. He was the opposite of Gary in every facet.

Caring where Gary was self-centered. Giving where Gary took. Grateful where Gary only blamed others.

Luke had promised they were in this together, but that was before he knew the truth about her. Before he knew she wasn't worthy.

She'd just given him the escape he might not have even realized he was looking for. And he'd be a fool not to take it.

With a slow lick of her lips, she risked a glance toward him. Luke's blue eyes blazed with something unreadable, but the intensity could not be mistaken. *Dear Lord, please don't let that be disgust.*

Anything else she could handle. No one could berate her more than she had already chastised herself. He couldn't say words of censure that she hadn't already screamed in the mirror.

But repulsion. The very idea that he'd be repelled made

her shudder in her seat, curling into herself, her arms crossed over her chest.

Suddenly his head jerked toward a dark sedan driving slowly by them. He watched it for far too long, saying nothing.

Without looking as if she was studying him, she tried to gauge the tension in his shoulders, to read the emotions in the lines of his body. But he was a blank slate.

Maybe she'd been wrong. Repulsion wasn't the worst reaction he could have. Indifference was far more painful.

It jabbed at her middle like a knife, and she reached for the door handle. She could just get out and go. She could call a cab and go back to the hotel and stay there until all of this blew over. Until whoever was after her had given up. Until she didn't have to deal with her memories. Until Luke wasn't part of her life.

Suddenly she couldn't breathe. Like an elephant had taken a seat on her lungs, she couldn't get any air in or out. And the tears had started in earnest, rolling down her cheeks and falling onto her lap.

And then, Luke hooked a finger around her hair, brushed it out of the way and tucked it behind her ear. With the same finger, he tipped her chin in his direction, forcing her to look at him.

If he looked closely, he'd see that she was crying, and then what? Pity?

Oh, who was she kidding?

He'd certainly already noticed her emotional overflow. It was time to face the music.

She gave a very unladylike sniff and scrubbed her hands over her face. With a shake of her head, she looked him square in the eye.

"I'm glad you told me, that you trusted me with the truth." A light filled his eyes, making them shine even in the relative darkness of the car, and it made her stomach do a slow barrel roll. "Do you trust that I'll tell you the truth, too?"

She couldn't get the words out, so she gave him a slow nod, chomping into her quivering bottom lip.

"I don't believe that you're that woman anymore. Are you?"

Again, the words wouldn't find their way out of her throat, so she settled for a shake of her head.

"I know you're not. I watched you serve the children at the carnival, and I've seen the way you care for your patients. You're not at all the person you described." Luke's gaze flicked over his shoulder, as headlights from a passing car illuminated them. But when he looked back in her direction, his eyes were filled with compassion. Uncompromising empathy. "Why is it so much harder to forgive ourselves than it is to forgive someone else?"

"I don't know." She managed a shaky breath. "But I hate what I did."

"That's fair. Just don't hate yourself in the process. When we ask for God's grace, we get it. You've got to accept that and keep moving forward."

His words washed over her like a Southern California winter rain.

Had she missed out on real mercy because she'd been too wrapped up in her own shame?

True grace wiped away sin and tore down prison walls.

But it didn't always remove the consequences.

And at the moment, the cost of her choices could be her life.

Luke moved his thumb to her cheek and started to wipe away her last tear, his fingers infinitely tender. But suddenly he dropped his hand to his lap, his expression tinged with sadness.

"Thank you." She couldn't look into his eyes a moment longer and dropped her gaze to his Adam's apple.

"You don't have to—" She licked her lips and tried again. "You could have sent me… That is, you don't have to be so nice to me."

"We've been over this. More than once. When I said that we are in this together, I meant it. You can keep trying to push me away all you want. I'm not going anywhere until I know you're safe. For good."

Between the gas at her house, her confession and his kindness, her nerves were threatening to mutiny. Time to go.

She grabbed the door handle and stepped onto the curb before he could say something else to make her cry. He followed her, crossing the squishy grass toward the front door. "You're sure your parents won't—"

He held up a hand to halt her, just as the dark four-door car crept around the corner for a fourth time. Her pulse skittered as the hair on her arms stood on end. Someone was watching them. Even here. Was there nowhere safe?

The minute its headlights lit them up, the car picked up speed.

"Wait here." Luke ditched his crutches and ran toward the street with an uneven gait, but the car was nearly to the far corner already. As he stepped off the curb, his knee gave way, and he crashed to the ground with a cry that pierced the night.

TEN

Luke bit back the scream on the tip of his tongue, grabbing for his leg as he fell. He tucked into his right side, letting his shoulder take the brunt of the blow against the ground. He grunted as the impact knocked the air out of him.

Almost before he realized he'd hit the pavement, Mandy was there, her cool hands running along his arms and down to his knee. "Did you twist your knee? How much pain are you in?"

He sucked in two quick breaths and squeezed his eyes closed, taking an assessment of his injuries. "My shoulder hurts worse." He squinted up at her, but she didn't even notice, her full attention on his brace, which had kept him from twisting his knee. And had also kept him from chasing down the car that, by his count, had driven around the block at least four times.

Of course, he'd known he couldn't outrun the vehicle, not even at his physical peak. But he'd hoped for at least a look at the license plate or a chance to make out the model of the dark sedan.

Instead he'd landed on the ground in a useless pile.

Watching out for Mandy gave him a direction, a purpose that he desperately needed. But with an unsteady leg, which still couldn't walk more than a few minutes without aid, maybe he was more hindrance than help. Maybe at quarter speed he was just holding her back from identifying her stalker.

No.

He silenced the voice of doubt with a firm shake of his head. He couldn't dwell on that thought. He wouldn't. No matter if there was more than a touch of truth to the qualms ringing through his mind.

Pushing his hands against the asphalt, he sat all the way up, meeting Mandy's frazzled stare for an instant. She tugged on his brace to make sure it was still tight around his leg, and it only pulled his pants askew.

"Did your knee buckle or just give out?"

She was in full-on doctor mode, and he managed to meet her grim expression with a half grin. Maybe if he played it off a little, she wouldn't ask more questions, wouldn't get the embarrassing truth out of him. "I'm okay, Doc. I didn't twist it. There was just a bit of pain that I wasn't expecting."

"Was it sharp, like something tearing?"

"No." He bent his good knee and tried to push himself up, but she kept an immovable hand on his shoulder.

Her nimble fingers traced around the opening of his brace at his kneecap. "It doesn't feel swollen yet, but let's get an ice bag on it just in case."

He nodded, quick to agree to anything that would get him off the ground and out of her line of questions. "Sure. Sounds good. Let's go inside."

"Before we move you, when you fell, where did it hurt?"

He shrugged a shoulder and stabbed his opposite hand through his hair. "It's fine. I'm good."

The streetlight poured over her shoulders, turning her hair into burnished bronze and setting her face in the shadows. He couldn't read her expression, but the slump of her shoulders suggested she was disappointed in him.

She'd warned him to be careful. More than half a dozen times. They both knew what it would mean if he tore those ligaments again. Even in the cool San Diego night, sweat rolled down his back. The very thought of never returning to the teams had him shaking with frustration and something too close to fear for his liking.

She let him sit for a long moment before asking a quiet question. "Why'd you go after that car?"

He looked in the direction of where it had disappeared. "It was circling the block."

"I know. I saw it, too."

His gaze snapped back to her face. "You did?"

"Of course. Now, let's try getting you up." She lifted his arm, draped it over her shoulders and wedged herself against his side. Every place she touched sparked to life, and he had to force himself not to lean into her nearness. Hadn't she just told him about her fiasco with a patient? She hadn't exactly come right out and said it, but she'd been clear. Getting involved with a patient wasn't going to happen. Even if he was the patient.

He was pretty sure that was why she'd told him about Gary and Camilla.

She had put up a wall between them. No matter how close they had gotten. No matter how many kisses he'd almost given her.

No matter how much he disagreed.

But he wouldn't push her. He wouldn't break those barriers. She had her reasons. Even if they were mostly built around her own insecurities.

She worried that she'd repeat her mistakes.

But he didn't. He'd known her for less than two weeks, and he knew deep inside that she wasn't capable of hurting someone like that. He just had to help her see that she'd changed.

Mandy slowly moved to a squatting position, hoist-

ing him up on his good leg. When he was standing, she
wrapped an arm around his waist, and he assumed that
meant it was okay to leave his hand on her shoulder, which
was good. Without her he wasn't going to make it back to
the front steps.

"I can call your orthopedist right now, and we can get
you scheduled for an MRI."

He squeezed her shoulder and chuckled as they hobbled
across the lawn, favoring his left leg. "I don't need to get
checked out. I didn't hurt my knee."

"How can you be so sure?"

Well, there was just no getting around it now. "I went
down because I got a leg cramp."

She stopped; so he did, too. And when she looked up
into his face, the porch light reflected in her eyes. Gone
was the remorse that had filled them before, replaced now
by humor.

"So the big, bad navy SEAL got taken down by a cramp."
She covered her mouth, but it couldn't cover her snort.

And somehow it was the sweetest sound he'd ever heard.
His stupid stumble was worth it if it could make her smile
after a night like this. If he couldn't physically rescue her
from the threat, at least he could be there for her to lean
on in the darkest hours.

"Let's just go inside." He pushed open the big wooden
door and motioned for her to walk into the foyer, where
his parents had undoubtedly been eagerly waiting to meet
her, if his mom's clasped hands and glowing face were
any indication.

His mom was a petite woman, shorter even than Mandy,
and she scurried across the hardwood floor, her hand outstretched. "Oh, you must be Mandy. Luke has told us all
about you."

Mandy shot him an elevated eyebrow, which made him

choke on a laugh, before reaching out to shake his mom's hand. "Mrs. Dunham. It's very nice to meet you."

"Oh, call me Sharon. And this is Ken." She reached back to tug on her husband's arm. When he stepped forward, his greeting was warm but not brimming with the expectations that seemed to fill Sharon's every syllable.

"The house has been so quiet since Luke joined up, and now we have two houseguests. It's so good to have him back. And with a *friend*." Sharon nearly glowed, leaning heavily on the last word, clearly hoping that they were much more than that.

She could hope all she wanted. Luke could, too, for that matter. It wasn't going to change what Mandy had said in the car.

She didn't want his pursuit. She didn't want him.

And he would figure out how to respect that.

Somehow.

"You must be starving." Sharon motioned toward the back of the house and the gourmet kitchen there. "Let me make you some dinner."

Mandy pressed a palm over her mouth, and Luke cut in. "Mom, it's been a long night. Mandy probably just wants to get some rest." As if on cue, Mandy nodded. "I'll give her a quick tour of the house. Could you find some pajamas for her?"

"Of course." Sharon scampered off and disappeared up a carpeted staircase.

His father, in typical fashion, kept his words brief and his grin gentle. "You kids have a good night. Let us know if you need anything." With a clap of Luke's shoulder, he said, "Good night."

"Good night, Dad."

When he was well out of earshot, Mandy let a chuckle escape from behind her hand. "Kids? I can't remember the last time someone called me a kid."

Luke shrugged. "I haven't lived here since I was eighteen, but I've got to say there are some perks to being at home. Like my mom's cooking."

"Good?"

"The best." He took off for a room on the far side of the spacious entryway, his crutches clattering with every step. "If you need me, I'm staying in here." He pushed the door all the way open to reveal a large office with a mahogany desk in the center of the room. Rows of matching bookshelves lined the far wall, and a big window overlooked the gentle neighborhood hills.

"You're sleeping in here?" She ducked her head into the room, her gaze falling on the therapy equipment lined up next to the single bed that had displaced the leather sofa.

"All the bedrooms are upstairs, and I'm not great with the stairs. That's why I moved back in the first place. My apartment is on the third floor, and I couldn't make that hike the first couple weeks after surgery."

"And now?"

"I could probably make it." He shrugged. "But the food is way better here."

"You're such a guy." She rolled her eyes and caught the reflection of a row of padlocks along the windowsill. She did a double take to see what they were attached to, but they weren't connected to anything. "What are the locks for?"

He shrugged. "Just a hobby."

"Here are some pajamas you can borrow." They both swiveled as Sharon announced her return, arms laden with plaid flannel. "And I brought an extra blanket just in case. The guest room can be kind of drafty."

Mandy accepted the armload and hugged it to her chest. "Thank you."

"My pleasure, honey." Sharon stepped in to give Mandy a hug, and a surge of jealousy spiked through Luke. That should be his move. "You're welcome here as long as you need a place to stay."

After Sharon had wished them sweet dreams and he'd pointed out a few other things in the house, Luke took Mandy to the base of the stairs that led to the guest room above the garage.

"Your room is right up there. There's an attached bath and plenty of clean towels and everything else."

"Thank you." Her chin dipped, her hair falling forward.

He reached to tuck a lock back in place but stopped short. Forcing his hand back to the grip of his crutches, he took a little step away. Away from the sweet smell of her shampoo. Away from her warmth. Away from the need to hold her close.

"You've really been... You don't have to be this nice to me."

"I know." And just like he'd hoped they would, his words brought her flashing brown eyes sailing upward. "But I want to."

The lightning in her eyes faded, replaced by a quiet determination. "I won't be here very long. We're going to find her. And then I'll be out of your hair."

"Yes, we will." He had to choke out the words as a strange weight settled on his chest. "We'll start into those files tomorrow."

She nodded, then walked up the stairs, the door closing behind her with a quick snick.

He could only wait for the vise around his lungs to release. Because they would figure out who was after her. She would be safe again. And when she was, he'd have to let her go. When she wasn't in danger and his therapy sessions ended, there'd be no excuse to see her, no reason to reach for her hand.

He needed her safe.

And he needed her in his life.

* * *

"Another pancake, honey?"

Mandy looked up from her seat at the kitchen table the next morning and tried to speak around the enormous bite of cinnamon-blueberry perfection already in her mouth. "Yeth. Pleath." She held up her plate, and Sharon scooped up two more perfectly round pancakes with a wink.

"Got any more for me?" Luke sat across from her, a smudge of sticky syrup stuck in the corner of his smile. He looked at his mom, then back at his empty plate, his grin turning on the charm.

Sharon squinted at him as Mandy shoveled in another pancake. "You've already had seven."

He shrugged and gave it another try. "I'm still growing."

Both Mandy and Sharon snorted at that. "Maybe your nose," Mandy said, slicing another wedge off her breakfast and dunking it into real Vermont maple syrup.

That got a chuckle out of both Luke and his mom, and Sharon patted her on the shoulder. "I like this one."

Luke nodded. "Me, too."

Mandy locked eyes with him over the butter dish. Like a feather running down her spine, his gaze left her tingling all over and desperate to ask him what he meant by that. But she couldn't force the words out. Not when the results were a lose-lose.

Either he meant his feelings for her were growing well beyond where they should be. And she'd have to let him down.

Or he only meant that he liked her as a friend and was concerned for her safety. And then she'd have to hide how much that hurt.

There was just no winning if she asked him to clarify.

Her only hope was to figure out who was after her and then make a clean break.

She dropped her gaze back to her half-eaten pancakes

and downed them in two bites, chewing as fast as she could and ignoring the weight of Luke's gaze on her. As soon as she swallowed the last morsel, Sharon swept through and picked up her plate, refilled her orange juice and cleared the rest of the table.

Mandy risked a peek at Luke. "I feel like I'm seventeen again. No one's taken care of me like this in ages."

"Isn't it great?" Her surprise must have registered on her face because he chuckled. "Not forever, but just for a few days, it's kind of nice. Besides, Mom thrives on this."

"Well, if she doesn't want me here forever, then we better dig in." Tugging on the edge of the box that she'd taken from her office, she pulled it across the table and reached in for a stack of files.

He attempted to grab some documents, as well, but she stopped him with a hand on top of his. "These are still patients, and I can't share their medical records."

His eyebrows furrowed, but then he nodded, stood and limped across the room. Picking up a laptop from the built-in desk beside the kitchen, he carried it back to the table. "You give me names. I'll do some reconnaissance."

She paused for a split second, weighing the nuances of the law that protected her clients with the need to protect herself.

Well, she wouldn't reveal anything about these cases beyond their names. The rest of the information they needed would come from public records. It was the best she could do, given her circumstances.

Luke settled in next to her, opening the laptop, his eyebrows raised in anticipation.

"All right." She pulled a folder out and flipped through it, searching for any words or phrases that might indicate the patient hadn't been very happy. On the third file, a note caught her attention. *Dr. Thurston recommends slow-*

*ing therapy down. Suggests incorporating more rest be-
tween sessions.*

And three lines later, *ACL torn again.*

Her stomach twisted, but she managed to push the feeling away and flipped to the front page. Douglas Rinnoco.
"This one. He's the one who pushed too hard and reinjured
his knee."

Luke's fingers poised over the keyboard, he asked, "His
name?"

"*R-I-N-N-O-C-O.* Douglas Rinnoco."

With a nod Luke went to work while Mandy sifted
through more patient files, praying that none of the pages
represented the person trying to kill her. And alternately
hoping that they might break her case wide-open.

After several minutes, Luke swiveled the screen in her
direction. "Is this him?"

The gray eyes that, during their sessions, had reminded
her of steel stared back her. "Yes. Where is he? What's
he doing?"

"He's some sort of financial consultant in Phoenix." He
clicked to another page that featured Doug's biography. "It
says he started with this company three years ago."

Mandy leaned back, realizing how close she'd gotten
to Luke's shoulder. "So… He's not the one?"

"I doubt it. I mean, we should still ask Fletcher to look
into him. But it would be a pretty big feat for him to be
stalking you from another state. Besides, it looks like he's
moved on with his life."

She let out a slow breath, trying to school her features
against the disappointment that made her chest ache and
pulse throb. She hadn't exactly expected this to be easy,
but she'd hoped for a break. This wasn't it.

Luke navigated to another website and pointed to a
picture of a girl walking on two new prosthetic legs. Her

smile stretched wider than her face as she looked up into the eyes of a man with dark hair.

"Any chance this is the girl whose dad was so upset that you couldn't help his daughter get new legs?"

Mandy's mouth hung open as she pulled up the distant memory. "How on earth did you find her?"

Luke shrugged. "I figured if her parents didn't have the money for what they wanted, maybe they'd look for an organization that could help." Clicking over to the home page, he pointed to the foundation's logo. "This local group helps financially strapped patients pay for prosthetics."

The caption below the picture said these were Bethany's first steps, and the joy on the girl's face left Mandy blinking against a sudden dampness in her eyes.

"Bethany Woolsly. That's her."

Luke stared at Mandy for a long moment, and she had to look down to brush away the tears.

"That just leaves the girl from the car accident." He nodded toward the stack of files on the table that was now bigger than the one inside the box. "Any luck?"

She shook her head and dug back in.

The second-to-last record had the case she remembered, and she held her breath as she flipped through the pages. Her notes were sparse but clear. The patient wasn't ready to face the rigors of therapy, especially since the chance of walking again was almost none.

"Her name was Laney Tr-Tract." Mandy swallowed the emotion clogging her throat, blinking back tears that had swiftly morphed from joy to regret. "She was sixteen."

Luke didn't immediately turn back to his computer. Instead he inspected Mandy, his gaze almost tangible as it swept over her face. She pressed her hand to her cheek, unsure if she wanted to block his view or hold the sensation there. All too soon it was gone, his attention back on the screen.

It was better this way. He was helping her get closer to the answers she needed. She didn't want him staring at her, touching her, comforting her.

Right.

She'd keep telling herself that until she really believed it.

"There's a few Laney Tracts popping up around San Diego. Do you have her parents' names?"

Mandy turned back to the file, but it was useless. It didn't have the guardian's name or even an address or phone number. "Before we got Tara, our office wasn't the most organized. I'm afraid we don't have complete records for most of these cases."

Luke made a low hum in the back of his throat. "Maybe there's an article about the accident." Three minutes later, he tapped his finger against the tabletop. "There it is. Almost four years ago Laney Tract of Vacerville was paralyzed in a one-car accident. It says here that the driver of the car was Laney's sister, but she's not identified by name."

"I suppose that's enough to pass along to Detective Fletcher." She reached for her phone, then dialed the police station as Luke began typing again.

"This is Fletcher." The smooth voice on the other end of the line sounded more like it belonged to a radio DJ than a salty detective.

"It's Mandy Berg."

He jumped in before she could continue. "I don't have any new information for you, Ms. Berg. We're working on getting a warrant for Mrs. Heusen's financial records, but these things take time."

"I understand. But I've been thinking—wondering, really. What if Camilla isn't the one after me?"

Something squeaked loudly on the other end as if his chair had protested a sudden shift. "Do you have any idea who it might be?" His pen tapped a rapid rhythm.

"I have a few ideas based on cases that didn't turn out quite like I had hoped." She laid out the relevant information from her files and from what Luke had found while the detective offered mumbled words of encouragement for her to continue.

By the end of her story, Fletcher let out a long sigh. "Looks like we might have another suspect. Or at least a motive. The first two are pretty thin, but the Tract girl's family might be looking for some retribution. I'll look into it."

"Thank you."

After Mandy hung up, Luke propped his chin on steepled fingers. "So?"

"He's going to check it out."

Luke nodded. "That's good."

She couldn't help the shivers that ran down her arms, despite the long sweater covering them. "But is it enough?"

With a barely perceptible shrug and tilt of his head, he seemed to ask the same question of her. "I found an address for the Tracts in Vacerville."

"You did?"

He nodded. "We could go check it out. See if anyone from the family still lives there."

Her heart thumped. Hard. She could be only an hour's drive away from discovering if this family had held a grudge against her. "Let me get my purse."

ELEVEN

The Vacerville city-limits sign might have been pretty twenty years before, but the unrelenting California sun had left the blue and yellow paint faded, the wood splintered and cracked. Someone had swerved off the two-lane highway, fracturing the right support post. And that sign was the best-looking part of the town.

Luke slowed as they rolled down Vacerville's main street, which was lined with boarded-up shops and dirt-caked storefronts. A crooked sign for the *Vacerville Gazette* flapped in the wind over the only lit window in the row. The once-thriving community seemed to have lost its heart. And most of its citizens.

Even the post office boasted a closed sign and directions to the next town over.

"What happened here?" Mandy pressed her fingertips to the passenger window, looking over her shoulder at him. "It's like everyone just up and left."

"I don't know. But maybe it's better outside town." It couldn't be much worse.

The only evidence that they weren't alone was a cloud of dust in his rearview mirror.

There wasn't much improvement as he turned down a side street toward the Tracts' address. Blocks away from

Main Street, every yard boasted a for-sale sign, and nearly half had been foreclosed on.

If this was the world that Laney Tract had grown up in, he wasn't surprised that she'd struggled to find hope after the accident. It was hard to find after any injury. How much more so in a place that seemed to be caked in dirt and desertion?

He glanced down at his knee and then back up at Mandy's profile.

He'd been there—at the bottom of a well, grasping for any promise for the future and coming up short. He'd thought his world was over. Certainly the only future he'd ever dreamed of. The only one he'd ever wanted.

And then Mandy had showed up. Like a light in a cave, her smile had reached to his very darkest places and given him a glimpse of the life he could have. Even off the teams.

Just then, she shot him a sad smile, and his heartbeat hitched at her quiet beauty. She wasn't stunning like Bianca or simply cute like some of the girls who followed SEALs around. Mandy's big brown eyes, filled with compassion, warmed him all over. The soft curve of her lips reminded him of the missed opportunity to kiss her. The one he knew wouldn't come around again. The one that was far too easy to think about.

Forcing his gaze away from her and onto the houses lining the street, he pulled into the gravel driveway of a faded yellow ranch house that matched the number on his piece of scratch paper. It didn't have a for-sale sign under the big ficus tree in the front yard, but it also didn't look loved. The screen door hung on just the upper hinge, and no one had bothered to fix two broken-out windows in the sunroom.

"Should we see if someone's home?"

Mandy twisted the edge of her shirt before giving a curt nod. She slammed her door and was up the sidewalk before he could even get his crutches out of the backseat. She lifted her hand to rap on the doorjamb but stopped when she realized he wasn't at her side.

"I'm coming." He grumbled at his crutches, wishing he could count on his leg to hold up for longer than a few minutes. But he wasn't going to venture far without them after the tumble he'd taken the night before.

When he reached the front of the home, he pressed a finger to his lips and leaned in against the door.

Nothing.

Then suddenly a creaking floorboard.

He jerked away. "Someone's moving in there."

She nodded her understanding but suddenly spun in a slow circle, her chin pointing down the road. "Do you feel that?"

Before she even finished the question, he knew exactly what she meant. The weight of someone watching them was almost tangible, like fingers skimming along his spine. Goose bumps exploded down his arms and beneath his jeans. Making fists with both hands, he forced himself to take a slow inhale and hold it for three long seconds. When he finally exhaled, he was back in control.

"No one's going to attack us in public in broad daylight." He pointed at the door. "Go ahead."

Mandy's forehead wrinkled in question, but she did as he indicated. Her fist banged on the rickety door three times, and for a moment, it looked as if the door might crash to the ground under the unexpected abuse. He tugged her arm until they were both out of the way of the swaying wooden frame.

Still no one answered.

Luke motioned toward the edge of the house, keeping his voice low. "Let's check the window."

Mandy led the way, staying close to the building and making hardly any noise. Almost as if she'd snooped around before. "You've been holding out on me," he whispered. "You're pretty good at this."

"I've been practicing." She attempted a moment of levity, but beneath the teasing twinkle in her eye lay a foundation of fear. The muscles in her neck grew tense, and she clenched her jaw.

He cupped her elbow just as they reached a shoulder-high window. "It's okay. No one in there—or out here—is going to hurt you. I won't let them." But a hook in his stomach made him pause.

Sometimes he couldn't control the outcome. He couldn't promise her safety.

She released a slow breath, which he took for agreement. Her gaze shot from him to the window and back again, then she closed her eyes and lifted her face to the sky. He pinched his eyes tight and did the same. *Lord, keep us safe. And please let us find something helpful.*

His prayers had been sparse—at best—since the bombing. It was easier to imagine that God didn't care about him than it was to believe He'd allowed the injury that threatened everything Luke held dear. But somehow, working the most personal mission he'd ever been assigned had left him with nowhere else to turn.

Not that he wanted somewhere else to turn.

Mandy pinched the edge of the windowsill and pushed herself up on her tiptoes to get a peek into the house, so he followed suit, although he didn't have to strain for a good view. There wasn't much to see inside anyway.

From their vantage point the entire living room was deserted. A TV tray and folding chair were set up in the far corner, pointed toward a spot where the television might once have been. The windows were bare of curtains, the walls blank, white slates.

Suddenly two yellow eyes glowed from the edge of the

hallway. Mandy squeaked and grabbed for his arm as a masked rodent meandered across the living room.

Luke covered his laugh with his other hand. "I guess now we know who was in there. Just a raccoon."

"What're you doin' here?"

The unfamiliar voice right behind them made both Luke and Mandy jump, and they clambered around to face a man in bib overalls and a faded blue-and-white trucker hat. A greasy rag hung out of his front pocket, and he snatched at it without looking away from them.

"I asked ya a question."

Mandy blinked several times and pressed a hand to her chest as if her heart might burst if she didn't hold on to it.

Luke found his voice first. "Do you know the family that lived here?"

"The Tracts? Sure. Everyone on this street knew 'em. 'Specially the last few months they were here." The man's gaze took in Luke's crutches as if he was assessing the threat level. "You friends of theirs?"

"I'm Luke." He reached out to shake hands, but the other man's gaze remained cautious.

"I'm Mandy. I met Laney Tract a few times and was hoping to reconnect with her family."

The man's eyes turned sad, previously invisible wrinkles around the edge of his face jumping to light. "Little Laney." He sighed and looked down at the toe of his work boot, which he twisted into the grass. "She was a sweet girl. Before."

Before the accident. Before her future had been stolen. Before everything changed.

He didn't have to say the words. But somehow they rang through Luke's chest, calling him to cling to the hope that he'd found again. "Have you seen her parents?" Mandy asked.

"Nah. Her dad drunk himself into the plot right next to Laney's."

Luke and Mandy locked eyes for a split second. "Mr. Tract is dead?"

"Yup."

Mandy grabbed Luke's hand, her fingers digging into his. This was their only viable lead, and it was slipping away, no matter how hard she clung to him. He offered the only comfort he could, drawing loose circles on the back of her hand with his thumb.

"What about her mom?"

The neighbor scratched at the patchy whiskers on his cheek. "I'm not real sure. But they was in the papers a lot after the accident. The cops were out here nearly every night."

"Why?" The lilt in Mandy's word suggested she didn't really want to know, but she leaned forward, still holding on to Luke's hand.

The man scratched his stomach and sucked on a tooth with the tip of his tongue. "Well, the beer didn't help. There was always someone screaming like the roof was about to fall down." He lifted his cap and ran a hand over the bald spot on his head. "But mostly I think they was just sad."

Luke wouldn't have pegged the man as someone so perceptive, but he'd made a good point. A wounded bear lashed out. So did wounded people.

Reaching out his hand again, Luke looked right in the man's eyes. "Thank you for your time."

"Bud." He gave Luke's hand a tentative shake. "People 'round here just call me Bud."

Clearly deciding they weren't a threat, Bud wandered off, strolling down the street with his hands in his pockets and his grease rag flapping against his leg.

Luke kept his gaze on the man but leaned an ear toward Mandy. "He said the Tracts had been in the newspaper."

She straightened up. "I saw the office on Main Street. Think someone there might have kept up with them?"

"There's only one way to find out."

Mandy wrinkled her nose as she stepped through the door Luke held open. The home of the *Vacerville Gazette* reeked of damp paper and dust, its insides as dreary as its hometown. Pale walls looked as if the paint had just slid right off, and two fluorescent lights flickered from above a table just beyond the counter that separated the work area from the waiting room.

The only bright thing about the entire room was the young woman sitting behind the counter. Her nearly neon, orange hair could go toe-to-toe with Tara's, and her vibrant smile did more to light up the space than the sun peeking around drab shades.

At their entrance, the teenager jumped to her feet and leaned her elbows on the brown Formica. "Hi! You must be new to Vacerville. I know everyone in town, and we haven't met. I'm Gabby. Are you just visiting or here to stay? We sure have lots of houses available. Do you want to see the real-estate book?" She disappeared behind the counter, then popped back up with two copies of a home-buying guide, her words never stopping. "There's one for sale right by my house. It's a big blue one, and they just dropped the price again. Do you have kids? I'm a great babysitter."

Mandy took an extra breath, just to make up for the ones the girl had skipped in her deluge, and met Luke's grin with one of her own. Apparently the girl's name fit her well.

"We're actually looking for someone that used to live here." Luke had to interrupt her, or they might be stuck there all day.

The helium deflated from the girl's shoulders. "Oh."

"Do you know the Tract family?" Mandy did her best to keep her tone light and keep the girl talking. "Laney might have been a few years older than you."

A frown replaced the smile that had greeted them. "Of course I know who she was. Everybody does. The school counselor interviews all the students twice a semester to make sure no one's on the verge. It's like a warning story to keep us from getting too sad about how everything closed."

Mandy took a step forward and rested her fingers on the counter, right where Gabby's line of sight ended. "And why did everything close?"

"They took away our water."

Luke stepped up to her side. "The canal?"

Gabby nodded. "They said the farmers needed it more than we did, but without the water, the mill closed. And then people started leaving town. There's only seven families left here. Even the post office closed. Said it was cheaper to drive over from—"

"And the Tracts?" Mandy interrupted, figuring she wasn't going to get a chance to ask if she didn't. "Were they still here when the rest of the town started leaving?"

Gabby scrunched up her face as though she smelled something worse than moldy paper. "I guess they were gone already. 'Course, Mr. Tract was already gone, gone. After Laney, he was only around another six months before…you know. And Mrs. Tract, she just seemed lonely after that. She didn't wait for the mill to close. One day she was here, and the next her house was empty. That was maybe two and a half years ago."

"Do you know where she went?"

Gabby offered only a shake of her head, and Luke stepped forward with a cajoling smile, one that would have made Mandy tell him all of her secrets—if she hadn't already. "Is there anyone around who might have talked to Mrs. Tract before she took off? A reporter, maybe?"

Like a bee to pollen, the teenager leaned in toward Luke, a matching smile finding its way across her face. "Nope. We're closed except for deliveries on Sundays."

"So why are you here?" Mandy folded her hands in front of her, forcing them into submission, when all they really wanted to do was grab Luke's arm and tug him a few steps closer to her.

Except that was absolutely crazy.

Why was a teenage kid making her want to stake a claim that wasn't hers to make? She'd already made it clear to Luke that they couldn't be more than patient and therapist.

But her heart didn't seem to want to take the hint. So her head forced her to take a step away from him. He shot her a questioning glance out of the corner of his eye, never missing a thing. Mandy managed a wobbly smile and what she hoped was a reassuring nod.

"Oh, I'm behind binding up the daily papers for the morgue." She gestured to the giant book on the table behind her. The magenta cover was about three feet long and half as wide, and the newsprint pages were at least three inches thick.

"I didn't know anyone still bound up newspapers like that." Luke chuckled.

"Oh, Mr. Bitters—he's the publisher—he thinks that when he posts articles online the government is watching him." Gabby straightened the hem of her vibrant blue shirt and dropped her voice as if she thought her boss might be right. "So he won't start a website. We have to put all of the archived papers in the basement. In order by date. And Mr. Bitters is really particular about how they're stacked and preserved. He says it's the only record of what really happened in this town."

Mandy's gaze snapped to Luke's, and they both raised their eyebrows. He had to be thinking the same thing she was. There might be a useful story about the Tracts tucked away somewhere in the morgue.

Again, with his all-too-handsome self, Luke smiled at Gabby. "Any chance we could take a look at some of those old papers?"

She glanced at the clock on the far wall, then stared at the ceiling as if she was counting hours. "I guess. I'm only here for another forty-five minutes, though."

"That's all we need."

Mandy wasn't so sure they could wrap up their search that fast, but she wasn't going to argue the point. Forty-five minutes was a far cry better than no minutes. She followed Gabby and Luke toward a lonely door beneath the clock.

"I'll be up here if you need something." The girl flipped on a light at the top of a set of rickety wooden stairs. The yellow bulb was as effective as an umbrella in a hurricane, so Luke turned on the light on his phone.

On the top step he turned toward Mandy, and only then did she realize he didn't have his crutches with him. Without a thought, she reached for his arm. His responding smile was warm and knowing and just for her.

And it sent her knees shaking so badly she was afraid she'd have to lean on *him* to get down the stairs instead of the other way around.

He took an awkward stride, but she struggled to follow suit. Her toes edged out over the lip of the stair, but she couldn't seem to make them go all the way.

Luke leaned in so that he only had to whisper. "Are you okay?"

Clamping her mouth closed, she gave a jerky nod. "Mmm-hmm."

The tightening around his lips said he didn't quite believe her, but he kept moving.

Move your foot to the next step, Mandy. Just take the step.

When had she forgotten how to walk? She'd been closer

to him than this before. They'd shared more contact. More interaction. More emotion.

But somehow, holding on to him, inhaling the clean scent of his aftershave as they descended into a dank basement was more than all of that. And not nearly enough.

It was the latter that made her stomach churn.

This had to be enough. It did.

She didn't know how they made it all the way down without falling, but when he patted her hand around his elbow, she jumped away. Taking in the walls of gray metal shelves that lined every spare space, she did a slow circle. The giant newspaper books were just as Gabby had described, meticulously organized and extensive. Signs on each shelf identified the month and year of its contents, and Luke immediately moved to a stack from four years before.

When he picked up the first book, a cloud of dust billowed into the air, and he sneezed loudly.

"Bless you," she responded out of habit, and the dust settled on her tongue, making her gag.

Luke tossed the book onto a square table in the middle of the room. "Sorry."

Covering her mouth and nose with a cupped hand, she nodded. With her other hand, she flipped open the archives. Luke placed another of the tomes beside her and began scanning its pages. Taking Bud's tip, she checked the police blotter for the family's name in every issue, her eyes straining in the dim light. When she came up empty-handed in the first, she tugged another off the shelf, dust caking her shirt as she carried it over to the table.

Brushing her hands together, she flipped the second open. It was a bust, too. From Luke's lack of conversation, he hadn't been any more successful.

She was almost through the third book when she spied a familiar name.

Gregory Tract.

"I've got something."

"What?" Luke leaned over her shoulder, his chest bumping into her back, shooting sparks down each of her extremities and making her catch her breath.

She shoved aside the hyperaware sensitivity and read the short paragraph. "'Police responded to a domestic disturbance call Tuesday at 7:00 p.m. Gregory Tract of 501 Lichester Street was cited but not arrested. His wife, Ophelia Tract, declined to press charges. This is the third call to this address this month.'"

She twisted her neck to look at him but stopped when she suddenly had a perfect view of his lips. Swallowing required extra effort in the arid basement and twice that when her lips were mere inches from his. It wouldn't take much to reach them.

"Ophelia? Laney's mom?"

She had to clear her throat twice to get even a word out. "I suppose so.

"According to Bud, Gregory died, but what about Ophelia?"

"Gabby said—"

An enormous crash above them shook the ceiling so hard that dust rained into their hair. Mandy jumped, grabbing on to his biceps as he wrapped a protective arm around her waist.

"What was—"

Again she was interrupted. This time by the slamming door at the top of the stairs. As one, they scurried up toward it. Luke left a hand on her back as he followed her every step with an awkward lope of his own.

She grabbed the door handle, but it held.

"We're locked in." She gasped around the painful thumping of her heart.

Luke reached around her, confirming her diagnosis. "It'll be all right. Gabby must have forgotten about us." But there was a waver in his voice, confessing that he didn't really believe that. "Gabby," he called, pounding the heel of his fist against the door. "Is anyone out there?"

No response.

Putting on his fix-it face, he said, "Would you call the police?"

"Right." She pulled out her phone. Then stopped. "Do you smell something?"

His eyes grew wide. "It's gasoline." His nostrils flared. "And smoke."

Mandy froze, praying she'd misheard him. They were basically surrounded by kindling. The building would burn in a flash.

And they were stuck.

Because someone was still trying to kill her.

Luke waved his hand in front of her unseeing eyes. "Mandy. Call 911. Now."

She fumbled her phone as he jerked on the knob and slammed a shoulder into the door. But with his injury, he couldn't get the momentum he needed to break it open.

He pulled a strange knife out of his pocket. Not a typical Swiss Army knife, this one contained several picks, which Luke opened before trying them on the doorknob. He shook the handle again before inserting one into the lock and gently twisting it.

"Are you calling?"

"Yes!" Just as she finished dialing, a cloud of smoke seeped through the crack at the bottom of the door.

"Nine-one-one, what's your emergency?" The man on the other end of the line was crisp and clear.

Of course he was. He wasn't locked in a burning building.

Her heart hammering, she squeezed her phone in a sweaty palm and forced down the fear that threatened to choke her. "We're locked in a building that's on fire."

"What's your location?"

Her mind reeled with numbers and addresses. None of them helpful. "The *Vacerville Gazette*. I think we're on Main Street. Whatever that main road through town is."

"Can you get out?"

She whipped around to make sure she hadn't missed another exit. She hadn't. The smoke swirled around her knees, bounced around by the ceiling fan. "No. We're locked in the basement. At the newspaper. There's smoke coming in here."

"Okay. Help is on the way. They'll be there in a few minutes. Stay on the line with me."

Mandy nodded frantically as Luke, closer to the door, began to cough. Then he cried out, yanking his hand away from the handle as if it had burned him.

It *had* burned him.

The fire was right outside the door, and smoke was filling their space.

She tried to take a calming breath to clear her frantic thoughts but only choked on the black smoke that seared her throat. Its fingers reached into her lungs, clasping them until she was sure they'd burst. Her eyes smarted, filling with unshed tears, and she blinked against them. Fought hard against the panic rising from her middle.

They weren't going to make it. They weren't going to get out. They were going to die.

Oh, Lord. The short prayer was all she could muster as tears streaked down her cheeks.

"How much longer?" Luke asked, tracks of his own tears marring the soot on his face.

She fought the monster inside and managed a brutal croak. "How long?" she said into the phone.

"About ten minutes." The dispatcher didn't have to say more. She knew that like everything else, the emergency response team had been relocated.

But they didn't have ten minutes.

They didn't even have two.

She and Luke locked eyes for a brief moment, the thickening smoke making his figure fuzzy as the truth slammed into her. He was going to die, too. And it was all her fault. He would be collateral damage for whatever crime she'd committed.

And there was nothing she could do except beg for mercy.

Lord, save us!

TWELVE

Luke choked on the haze filling the landing. He hacked and coughed against the burning in his chest, the air itself painful.

Mandy leaned on the wall behind him, her back curled and head bent between her knees. She wobbled for a moment but kept her feet.

He spun back to the knob. He just had to get this pin to pop. It was clearly an upgraded lock, one the publisher had installed to keep Big Brother's prying eyes at bay, but it was still a pin-and-tumbler. It wasn't overly complex. Just enough to keep them from escaping.

He shut his watering eyes under the heat of the fire that licked against the other side of the door. When he did, he was in another place, another time. Eight years old and crying for help. Terrified and alone. Confined. Forgotten.

The memory made his skin too tight, as if it belonged to someone else, and he flexed his shoulders and back to stretch it out. That just made it feel as though it was on fire.

"God, we have to get out of here. Help us." His prayer was little more than a breath as he twisted his picklock one more time, hoping the pin would shift this time.

It didn't.

"Few more minutes," Mandy wheezed. "Fire department…few minutes away."

He risked a glance over his shoulder to find her skin sallow and her eyes red.

If Mandy lost consciousness, he couldn't carry her through the fire. He wasn't even sure he could get himself through it.

He glanced at the ceiling. *A little help. Please.*

The last pin slipped into place, and he released a long breath. "Get ready."

Mandy pushed herself off the wall, her movements sluggish. "Why?"

"We're going to have to make a run for it."

"You picked the lock?"

She didn't have to sound so surprised. He shot her a smug smile before covering his nose and mouth with the collar of his shirt. She followed his example, tucking her chin into her chest.

Letting go of his shirt for a moment, he held up three fingers. "Stay right by me. On zero." She jerked her head in understanding, and he ticked them down quickly. When he held up just a fist, he flung open the door, which pushed the flames apart just long enough for them to dash across the linoleum.

The fire licked at his arms, and his leg screamed at the light jog. But he pushed through.

Just keep going.

He zeroed in on the sunlight filtering through the front door. Fresh air and freedom were his only goal, Mandy's hand tucked tightly in his own. He kept her safe in the shelter of his embrace, acting as a wall between her and the blaze.

Escape was so close he could almost taste the cool water. They'd made it through the heart of the fire.

And then she tripped, taking two giant steps to stay upright, her fingers clinging to his. He spun and wrapped an arm around her to keep her on her feet.

"I'm okay."

He'd started to pull her toward the exit when he glanced down and saw what her foot had caught on.

Gabby.

She lay sprawled on the floor, her hair fanned out around her head, her breathing shallow.

"Keep going." He waved Mandy on. "Open the door."

She raced for the entrance as he grabbed Gabby under the armpits. Sweat poured down his back as he dragged the girl toward safety. His leg felt like rubber, every inch of him shaking. A spot on each forearm had been scorched by the fire, but he couldn't feel that pain yet.

And then a gust of fresh air swept around him. He stumbled onto the sidewalk and then the empty street.

He collapsed next to Gabby's still form, and Mandy fell down across from him.

The air was sweeter than water in Death Valley, and he angled Gabby's neck so she could drink deeply of it. But she didn't stir.

Suddenly sirens descended upon them, a fire truck and two ambulances taking up both sides of the street. And like ants from a flooded hill, emergency personnel poured into the street. When two paramedics reached Gabby, Luke scooted away. Usually he thrived in the thick of the action. He loved the adrenaline that pumped through his veins. He enjoyed using his medical training when it really counted.

But in that moment, staring at Mandy, he couldn't shake the feeling that he'd nearly lost the most precious thing in his life. Somewhere between a wild ride down a mountain road and hearing her panicked voice in the basement, he'd fallen for her. Hard. And ignoring it wasn't really an option. Of course, neither was acting on it.

"Ma'am, are you injured?" A young woman leaned over Mandy, who managed only a cough in response.

"She inhaled a lot of smoke." He sounded more toad than human. "Probably needs oxygen."

The paramedic's gaze shifted to him, her forehead wrinkling. "Javier! Javier!"

As soon as he saw the look in her eyes, the pain in his arms ignited. It was as if a switch had been flipped. The fading adrenaline opened the door for his nerves to cry out. Risking a glance down, he cringed. Each arm boasted a three-inch swath of seared flesh, and now that he noticed, the smell of charred hair nearly made him heave.

Javier approached at a run but stopped to survey his patient.

Luke probably had eight inches and fifty pounds on the guy, and with his knee brace and second-degree burns on his arms, getting him off the ground wasn't going to be easy.

But he wasn't about to get carted off on a gurney.

Holding up a finger, he croaked, "I can get up."

All of a sudden, Mandy was by his side, carefully wrapping his arm across her shoulders and circling his waist with hers. "All right. We've done this before. Just lean on me."

His chuckle turned into a roaring cough as she maneuvered him to his feet without twisting his knee.

"And maybe you should quit smoking. You don't sound so good."

He guffawed at that. "You're one to be talking, Smokey."

She helped him to the rear bumper of one ambulance as the other took off with Gabby in its bay. "Is she going to be okay?" Mandy pointed to the red beast rolling down the road.

"She got a bad knock on the back of her head and some smoke inhalation," Javier said, pulling out his medical supplies. "But she was regaining consciousness when I closed her in. Now let me take a look at your arms." After a thorough inspection, he reached around for a couple ice packs and put them on the burned areas. "Keep these on for about twenty minutes. Would you like to go to the hospital? These are small second-degree burns, but if you'd like, we can take you to the ER."

"No. That's okay. I'm a navy medic. I know what to do to care for these."

Javier nodded just as the young woman handed Mandy an oxygen mask. Luke let her put one on him, too, the green elastic band stretching around his head just above his ears.

He tried to breathe normally, but the unadulterated air was like a dessert buffet. Eventually he let himself close his eyes.

Just for a minute.

The shouts of firemen jerked him awake. Apparently he'd dozed off. The paramedics weren't in sight—though they'd almost certainly not wandered too far from their ambulance—and the firefighters were winning the battle against the smoking building.

Luke glanced at Mandy, her long lashes resting on now-pink cheeks. Just as he smiled, her eyes fluttered open. "Hey, you." His words were garbled by the mask, so balancing his ice packs, he pulled it down to his chin. "How're you feeling?"

After removing her mask, she returned his smile. "Better. You?"

"Good."

She raised a skeptical eyebrow.

"Fine. My arms feel like they're still on fire. And my leg feels like I ran a marathon, but I didn't twist my knee. Happy?"

She leaned her shoulder against his. "Yes." Resting her ear against him, her sigh was filled with every emotion he'd felt in the previous hour. "I'm sorry. I never meant for you to be caught up in all this," she said.

"I'm just sorry that I couldn't get that door open faster." Even now, he could feel his tools in his hands, searching for the pins. If the handle hadn't gotten so hot. If he hadn't lost the tension needed to keep the pins in place. If he'd just been a few minutes faster.

Then what? Then they'd be right where they were now.

Safe for the moment but nowhere closer to finding the person responsible.

"How did you know how to pick that lock? And you had that knife handy like you've used it a hundred times." Her jaw moved against his shoulder, but the touch wasn't enough. He shifted to let her lean her head against his chest, drawing her into his embrace.

The expectant silence prompted him to confess his unusual hobby. "When I was a kid, my mom would take me and my sisters up to my grandparents' place on the Oregon coast every summer. Just two weeks of running around barefoot and exploring the beach and the woods and Grandma's attic."

"Sounds wonderful."

"It was pretty great. But one summer, when I was eight, I found this old trunk in the attic with the key still in the lock. So I opened it up, and it had some old records and dolls in it. My dad had just read *Treasure Island* to me, and I was convinced there was a treasure in the bottom of that chest. But there were just a handful of dusty quilts. I was upset that there wasn't something more valuable, so I crawled inside to take a nap."

She nodded, as though validating his childish train of thought.

"I must have kicked one of the sides in my sleep because I woke up when the lid slammed shut. I was locked inside."

"Oh, Luke." The emotion in her voice matched the twist he felt in his gut every time he remembered that day. "How did you get out?"

"I screamed and yelled until I was hoarse, and no one

came. And I prayed and prayed that God would send someone to rescue me. But after what felt like hours, I was still trapped in there. I could see through the keyhole, but the key had fallen out." He pinched the bridge of his nose to relieve a tiny bit of pressure building there, all the fear still easily accessible. "I was hungry and so scared, and I think—as much as my eight-year-old self could—I realized that if no one ever found me, I was going to die. Alone."

Her hair swung across his arm, as she whipped her face in his direction. Her eyes glistened in the afternoon sun. "What happened?"

"My mom got really worried when I didn't show up for dinner." He rubbed his belly. "Even then I didn't like to miss a meal. And she came looking for me. When I heard her footsteps, I cried out, and she unlocked the trunk and let me out."

"Oh, Luke, I'm so sorry. That must have been awful."

He shrugged. "It wasn't so bad, really. Mom felt so horrible that I was in there all day, I got ice cream for dinner."

She gave him a playful elbow to the stomach, and he faked a pained wheeze.

"Honestly, it's a rough thing for a kid to face, but it gave me some purpose, too. I knew I wanted to do something with my life to help people who were trapped, who were facing death alone."

"That's why you became a SEAL?"

"Yep. It's also why I learned how to pick a lock."

She pulled away from him, twisting at the waist so she could look right into his eyes. "The padlocks in your room. You practice on those."

"I do."

She cupped his cheek with her palm, her touch like silk to his overheated skin. Underneath the scent of smoke, he could almost smell her sweetness. "Then I'm not sad you were locked in that trunk. Because of that, you saved us today. Because of that, you became a SEAL, who ended up at my practice. Who has saved me more times than I can count." She chewed into her lip. "I'm just sorry that you were so scared."

Her compassion stole his breath, and he pulled her closer. "I was more frightened today."

He heard Mandy's breath hitch, her unblinking eyes like pools of milk chocolate.

"I was afraid I was going to lose you."

"Me, too. And it was all my fault."

He brushed her hair out of her face, leaving his fingers behind her ear and closing the distance between them by half.

Somewhere, in the depths of his memory, he knew he wasn't supposed to be this close to her. He wasn't supposed to comb his fingertips through her hair. He most certainly wasn't supposed to kiss her.

His stomach dropped, and he threw away all caution.

She leaned into him, her lips soft beneath his. Her hand whispered to the back of his neck, playing with the shaggy curls there. Wave upon wave of goose bumps rolled down his back, and he couldn't stop. Quite honestly, did not want to.

He just wanted to be closer to Mandy. Safe in her arms.

She made him feel protected. He was supposed to be the protector, but somehow she was the one who gave him the courage to keep fighting in spite of his injury. In spite of his uncertain future. She gave him a purpose and a reason to keep going.

The world seemed to stop spinning, and everything disappeared.

Everything except Mandy and their perfect kiss.

Mandy had never known something so sweet, so powerful. Luke's kiss was like lightning over the Pacific. It made everything inside her jump to attention, her every hope and dream suddenly illuminated.

She tried to breathe but couldn't. And the air that had been so precious just minutes before was now overrated, unnecessary.

Twining her fingers into his ruffled waves, she held on for all she was worth, letting him be both her undoing and her anchor. His arms—even injured—were unrelenting, gentle but unmovable.

Resting his forehead against hers, he snuck a quick breath, and her smile felt as if it would crack her cheeks. When he swooped in for another kiss, her stomach took flight, soaring without concern. And taking her with it.

This kiss was like nothing she'd ever known before. Not as a teenager. Not as an adult. Not even with…

Who could think about *him* when Luke filled all of her senses? He filled her heart with a joy that no other man had sparked.

This moment was near perfection.

And then it was rudely interrupted.

The cop tried to be subtle, clearing his throat and offering a fake cough. But it had the same result.

Mandy jumped away from Luke, her cheeks burning and lips tingling as sense tumbled back into place.

She'd told him they couldn't share anything more than what they had. She'd told him why she needed space. And then she'd very nearly attacked him. How many mixed messages could a girl give?

Luke's eyes were hooded but still shone with a combination of pleasure and pain. Or was it confusion? She couldn't tell, couldn't concentrate when he pressed his thumb to the corner of his mouth, and all she wanted in the world was to have him touch her lips again.

Get ahold of yourself, Mandy!

But screaming at herself wasn't going to help. She'd

crossed the line that she'd drawn, broken the promises that she'd made.

Again.

Didn't she have any self-control? A handsome, kind, protective, compassionate man walked into her life, and she suddenly forgot all her rules.

No. This could not happen again. It just couldn't.

Except, the butterflies in her stomach suggested that all she really wanted was a replay.

Before the not-so-patient officer could capture their full attention, Luke whispered, "I'm so sorry."

His words were a knife to her chest, and she had to ignore them as the cop said, "What happened here? Our dispatcher said you were locked in the basement when the fire started."

Mandy's eyes shifted between Luke—whose face seemed to say that they would talk more about this later—and the officer. She wanted to talk about what had just happened right now. Actually, that wasn't true. She wanted Luke to say he was sorry for saying he was sorry. She wanted to know that the kiss had meant something to him.

But if he felt otherwise, she most definitely did not want to know that.

Especially in front of the fidgeting officer.

Finally she focused on the cop with a hesitant nod. "We were looking at the archived newspapers when someone locked us in." She recounted the rest of their experience in sparse detail while the officer jotted down a few notes.

"And what were you doing down there in the first place?"

"Someone's been trying to kill me, and I think it might be related to a local family."

The cop shifted his stance, his pen frozen over his notepad. "Kill you?"

"Yes." It was surprisingly easy to say at this point.

Somewhere along this road, she'd come to terms with being hunted. It wasn't ideal. It was simply life as she knew it. Life for the foreseeable future—until the cops could find the person after her.

This time she told him everything. The almost hit-and-run, cut brake lines and gas leak. But as she reached Vacerville in her story, her words slowed, her brain churning. She closed one eye and looked into the sky, trying to pinpoint a nugget of information that danced just beyond her consciousness.

With a glance at Luke, she said, "There was something in that basement we weren't supposed to see."

Luke scrubbed his hands down his face, but when he met her gaze, she could see he was making the connection, too. "Whoever is after you followed us out here. She tracked us. She could have stayed in San Diego. We'd be back. But she knew that there was information out here that would point to her."

"She's never seriously targeted anyone except us, but she was willing to kill Gabby to keep us from finding whatever is—was—down there. All of this has to be related to Laney Tract." She flipped a hand toward the smoldering remains of the building. And now they'd never know. The archives were almost certainly a total loss, between the fire and water.

The officer kept taking notes, even as his eyebrows pulled together to create three deep lines above his nose. "Have you been talking to a detective in the city?"

She pulled Detective Fletcher's card out of her purse, and the cop told them he would be in touch if any evidence surfaced.

After the paramedics released them, Mandy helped Luke up, acting as his crutch as they crossed the street. "How's your knee? Really."

"Actually, it feels good. My quads are a little sore just from being used after such a long break, but there's no lingering pain in or around my knee." He squeezed her shoulder and winked. "Besides, I made sure I was on stable, even ground before running through that fire."

"Your physical therapist will be glad to hear that."

He gave her an obligatory chuckle as they settled on the road home, the sun setting just ahead of them. Several times he opened his mouth, shook his head and clamped it shut again. The seasick feeling in her stomach told her exactly what he was trying to say, and she didn't want to hear it. Not after a day like this. So when he finally started, "Listen, about earlier—"

She immediately cut him off. "So, Ophelia Tract. I guess we should be looking for her. I'll call Fletcher as soon as we get back."

Luke's gaze settled on her, heavy and knowing. But finally he nodded. "All right. I'll see if there's anything to dig up beyond the *Vacerville Gazette*."

"Good."

Even though nothing was.

THIRTEEN

Mandy woke the next morning to a ringing phone. Caught in a comforter cocoon, she thrashed around, trying to reach the offending duck call on the nightstand. Finally an arm broke free, and she snatched up her phone.

"Hello?"

"Mandy?"

"Tara?"

"Did I wake you up? You sound awful." Tara sounded surprised to have reached her boss.

Opening one eye, she looked around the unfamiliar room, trying to figure out where she was. She spied a shabby-chic Guests Are the Best sign hanging on the wall adjacent to the door. Right. She'd slept in Luke's parents' guest room once again. And after the terror of the fire the day before, it had been a deep sleep. "Sorry. Long story. There was a fire."

"Oh my. Are you okay?"

"Fine. I left you a message last night about having one of the assistant PTs cover my appointments today." After the day before, there was no way she could focus on her patients that morning.

"Yes, and Jesse is covering them for you. But…"

"What is it?"

"Um…well…" She paused for a long second. "Maybe

it's nothing, but I thought I saw Camilla outside the clinic yesterday."

That didn't make any sense. Whoever was after her most likely had a connection to Laney Tract—or she wouldn't have burned down the newspaper office. Camilla didn't have any link to Laney. Did she?

"Why were you at the office?"

"I forgot my beach bag." She laughed it off but then turned serious. "Camilla was sneaking around outside. I think she might have tried to break into the office if I hadn't been there. When she saw me, she took off."

This just didn't make sense, and it made her insides twist. Struggling her way out of the cocoon, she propped herself up on a mountain of pillows. "What kind of car was she driving?"

"I didn't get a good look at it. She must have parked around the corner."

"And you're sure it was Camilla Heusen?"

"Well, I mean, I haven't ever seen her in person, but she matched the description you gave the detective. Dark curly hair. Thin build. And a tattoo on her forearm."

The description fit, but where was the connection to Vacerville and the Tracts? And if she was in San Diego, then who had set the fire sixty miles away?

"What time did you see her?"

"It was early," Tara said.

Before they'd left town. Camilla would have had time to follow them.

"Thanks, Tara. I'll see you in the office tomorrow."

"Sure thing."

Mandy wrestled her way out of her covers and went to make herself presentable before clomping down the stairs. When she reached the kitchen, she had to lean against the door frame and gasp for air to bring her pulse to a reasonable rate.

At the table, Luke jumped up and rushed to her side. "What happened? Are you all right?"

"Tara just called. Camilla was at the office yesterday morning. Do you think she has a connection to the Tracts?"

He shook his head, ushering her to a chair. "I have no idea. Let me get you some water. Then you need to call Detective Fletcher. He has to follow up on Ophelia Tract."

After sipping the liquid for a few seconds, she called the police station. "Detective Fletcher is out of the office today," said the pleasant voice on the other end of the line. "Do you want to leave him a message?"

No. She didn't want to leave a message. She wanted answers and some help.

"Is there someone else I can talk with?"

"Let me check."

Mandy drummed her fingers on the table as she waited. While the unknown threatened to clog her throat, Luke poured over whatever he could find on the internet. His forehead wrinkled, and he scratched at his chin, his eyes shifting back and forth.

"Hello, this is Detective Boller."

"Hi, this is Mandy Berg. I've been working with—"

"Ray Fletcher. Sure. He told me about your case."

The band squeezing her chest eased up just a bit. They weren't really in this alone. Even if it sometimes felt that way. "Camilla Heusen was at my office yesterday."

"Are you sure about that?" Papers rustled, and Boller clicked his teeth together. "Ray has a note on his desk to follow up on a flight. It looks like Mrs. Heusen may have booked a flight to Rio de Janeiro."

"She left the country?" This puzzle was getting more convoluted by the minute.

"Possibly… It wouldn't be the first time that a suspect booked travel to give herself an alibi."

Sure. Of course. "Well, would you just let Detective

Fletcher know that either Camilla or someone masquerading as her was outside my office yesterday? Oh, and let him know I was caught in a fire at the *Vacerville Gazette* newspaper yesterday afternoon."

"Were you injured? Did you speak with an officer there?"

"I'm fine." She fished the uniform's name out of her purse and gave Boller the information. "I gave the officer Detective Fletcher's number, too. So he might have already called." She paused before dropping the big bomb. "And I think there's a connection to the Tract family. Gregory, Ophelia and Laney Tract from Vacerville. Can you look into them? Laney and her father have both passed away, but I don't know where Ophelia is."

Boller endlessly clicked the button on the top of his pen. "We'll see what we can find. I'll be in touch."

She hung up and put her face in her hands, her shoulders aching with tension.

"I think I found Ophelia Tract."

She jerked at his words. "Where is she?"

Luke spun the computer screen in her direction. "With the other Tracts."

Mandy's shoulders fell, and Luke covered her outstretched hand with his. The headline announcing Ophelia's obituary filled the screen, and it was more than two years old—shortly after she left Vacerville. The brief lines offered little more than her late husband's name and the time of the funeral.

"Another dead end," she sighed.

"Maybe not." Luke moved to another screen, which showed a picture of a row of headstones. Each boasted the name Tract, engraved in large letters at the top of the gray marble. But the names below the surname were smaller and hard to read in the grainy picture. She leaned in, squinting at the image.

"I don't see anything that can help us."

He pointed to the bottom corner of the stones. A small,

unreadable symbol seemed to be repeated on each one. "I'm not sure what it is, but I doubt it's a coincidence." He pursed his lips to the side and cocked his head. "Want to go check it out?"

"Absolutely."

By the time they got to the cemetery outside Vacerville, Luke had a sinking feeling that this had been a terrible mistake. He'd expected the country graveyard to be relatively small, but as he pulled into the parking lot beside a gray minivan, he realized the lawn before them was never-ending. Row upon row of markers lined the green grass for more than two hundred yards in every direction, and enormous oak trees dotted the landscape until they turned into thick woods. On the far right, a mausoleum touted a famous area resident. And outside the fence, a small house sat—if the toolshed behind it was any indication—for the caretaker. But far and wide, the simple markers that spanned the field looked very much like those from the online picture.

"Are we going to be able to get through this today?" Mandy echoed his doubts.

He held up a bag of snacks his mother had packed. "At least we won't go hungry."

She laughed and got out of the car. He followed her to the front gate, then glanced over her shoulder at the vehicle. His crutches were still lying in the backseat. When he secured the Velcro on his knee brace, he gave it a good tug. He could do this today. His leg felt better than it had in a while, especially after he'd gotten a good night's sleep.

With a nod to the left, he said, "I'll take this row."

Mandy looked to the right as the gravestones disappeared into a low slope. "Maybe I'll just take the next row up."

They strolled along under the late-afternoon sun, checking every plot for the familiar name. Several groups of grievers came to pay their respects, giving Luke and Mandy a wide berth. Always one row apart, they slipped around tree trunks, stopped to rest and then continued snaking their way through the cemetery as the sun began to sink behind the trees. Still they'd reached only half of the plots.

Looking up from the end of her row, Mandy surveyed the open field and wrapped her arms around her middle. He glanced around the now-empty cemetery, suddenly feeling very exposed. The clouds rolling over the pale moon rising in the distance weren't making him feel any better about being in such an open position. "Let's get out of here." Automatically he searched out patches of cover for their path back.

Just as he reached for Mandy's hand to keep her by his side, she jerked to a halt, pointing at three plots in a row. "Look. It's them."

Sure enough, just as the picture had showed, the three members of the Tract family were buried side by side.

Luke stooped to brush some dead grass from the top of Laney's marker, running his finger over the unusual symbol etched in the corner. "It looks Chinese, but I don't know for sure."

"Do you know anyone who would know?"

"Actually, I do. Tristan Sawyer is a linguistics expert. If he can't translate it himself, he'll know someone who can." He snapped a picture and sent it away with the flick of his thumb. Then he pushed himself upright, taking in the entire engraving: Beloved Daughter, Friend and Sister.

He sucked in a quick breath.

"What?"

"Laney's sister."

Mandy nearly crawled into his arms to get a better look

at it, flashing the light from her phone across the words. "That newspaper article online. It said her sister was driving the car when Laney was paralyzed."

How had they let that slip past them? It had been right there, but with so many other details, neither of them had paid any attention to it.

She leaned her head back and stared at the stars as if they could help make sense of a senseless puzzle. "Do you think— Could it be Camilla?"

Luke let out a low whistle. "That'd sure be some co-incidence."

Suddenly a car spun out in the gravel of the parking lot, its lights never flashing across the grass. A door slammed, and Luke's training kicked in. Like a warning siren, the lack of headlights signaled danger.

"We've got to go. Now." He grabbed Mandy's hand and took off for the nearest tree, his pulse already amped for a fight, his body reacting with muscle memory.

"What's happening?" She was out of breath already, but she held on to his hand as if it was a lifeline. Maybe it was.

He pressed her into the protection of the tree trunk, shielding the rest of her with his own body and peeking toward the parking lot. A shadow in all black dashed through the gate and then disappeared into the darkness. His stomach took a nosedive, and he rested his forehead against the rough bark just long enough to make a plan.

"We've got company."

"Camilla followed us?"

"She's been doing it for over a week. Always right behind us."

Mandy shook her head and pinched her eyes closed, dropping her voice. "But how? How does she know so much about—"

Suddenly a gunshot cracked through the night air, severing any hint of peace left.

"We're going to run."

"But how can you—"

"Don't worry about me. Just worry about holding on to my hand. Do not let go." He pressed his face in close to hers, locking onto her unblinking eyes. "Do you understand?"

"Yes." It was more squeak than word, but he'd take it.

"We have to get to better cover. That means the woods." Her gaze flicked toward the parking lot, and he felt the tug, too. How much easier would it be if they could just make it to the car and be gone? But the only way out was on the far side of an open field with a gunman shooting at them.

It didn't take a SEAL to know that was a death trap.

His heart thumped hard. Once. Twice. "Are you ready?"

With her nod, he tugged her into his side and began to run. When the second shot echoed across the lawn, Mandy jumped, nearly letting go of him. He just held on tighter, his legs pumping, feet pounding. Everything except the thought of protecting Mandy faded.

Another shot, this one closer. He could feel it rush past his cheek. Far too close for comfort.

They were just three steps away from the nearest tree. Two. One.

Bark exploded in front of him just as another report reached his ear. He veered left, toward the next oak. His foot slipped, and he winced as his knee threatened to buckle. *God, just keep me on my feet. Please.*

Two more shots followed them to the next tree. Then silence. Only the rustling of leaves in the spring breeze could be heard.

In his ear, Mandy gasped for air, the tree at her back most likely the only thing keeping her upright.

"Are you okay?"

She swallowed as if she hadn't had a drink in days but managed a nod. Her face was almost as white as her shirt, and he rued his own stupidity. She stood in stark contrast to the darkness, an easy mark for their pursuer.

Shrugging out of his overshirt, he wrapped it around her. His undershirt was just as white, but at least now he was the visible target and not her.

A twig snapped just on the other side of the tree, and his heart skipped a beat. Shutting out all his other senses, he listened carefully for the next noise. Only the barely there whisper of Mandy's breathing swirled around him. The rustling leaves in the branches above added to her song.

Finally a soft meow joined in.

Luke ducked around the base of the tree to stare directly into the glowing yellow eyes of a black cat. As the feline darted away, a human shadow raced toward them.

"Run." He took off, a surge of fear for her washing down his back as she stayed by his side.

His right foot hit a tree root, and he went down hard on his good knee. Swallowing the cry of agony that originated in his injured leg, he pushed himself up, Mandy tugging on his elbow. "Luke!"

Two quick shots split the air, and he forced himself to run through the pain. Just like SEAL training. All he had to do was keep moving through the pain. If he fell down, he'd stay down. And that wasn't an option.

But he couldn't do this for much longer. He'd only just started walking on his own.

God, I need Your help. I can't keep going. We need help.

As he zigged between two trees, a spotlight flooded the cemetery. A voice, aided by a bullhorn, seemed to shake his very soul. "Ain't you got no respect? You kids better stop with the fireworks. Now. Or I'll call the cops."

The caretaker.

Thank You, God.

Mandy sank against the nearest patch of bark, her head hanging forward as her shoulders rose and fell in rapid succession. Luke slid into place beside her but kept his view of the rest of the graveyard as he tried to swallow the lump lodged in his throat.

"There." He pointed. "Between the trees." The shadowed figure raced toward the entrance. A car door thumped, and an engine started. Down the road, the faint glow of headlights finally cut the night, and Luke leaned against Mandy's shoulder, resting his head on top of hers.

Her grip refused to loosen on his, and he pulled her around to face him.

In the darkness he could make out only the pale curve of her cheek and wide, wild eyes. Tracing the line of her jaw with one finger, he stopped at her chin, hitching it up.

"That was a close one," he whispered.

"Uh-huh."

"But you're okay. You weren't hit, were you?"

"Uh-uh." He assumed that was a no.

"Scared?"

She started to shake her head but stopped halfway and nodded vigorously.

"I know. Me, too."

She blinked twice. "You were?"

"I was. See?" He lifted her hand and pressed it to his still painfully thudding heart. "I've never been so scared in my life."

"Not even…" She looked down at his knee.

"Not even when that bomb exploded. I was ready to meet my Maker. I still am. But now I think about you, too."

Her fingers curled into the flesh over his heart, and he swallowed it with his own hand. His pulse wasn't going back to normal, his breathing wasn't evening out. This close to her, he could fly apart at any moment.

She tried for a smile and settled for half of one.

His stomach felt as if he'd stepped in a rubber boat on

the ocean for the first time. Every breath was a wave crashing against his bow. Every inch away from her, a mile.

All he really wanted was one more perfect moment.

But she'd been so clear about not being involved with a patient. As long as she was his PT, she couldn't be more.

Of course, he'd already crossed that line. Big-time.

And he wouldn't do it again. He wouldn't ask her to bend her convictions or make her doubt that choice. It was a solid one.

Even if it shouldn't apply to him.

Because he was in love with her.

He pressed his forehead to hers and let out a relieved sigh. Knowing that, admitting it to himself, granted him a freedom he hadn't known before. No matter the crutches he used or the braces he had to wear or the therapy he had to endure, he loved Mandy Berg.

And he'd wait until she was ready to love him back.

Pulling away, he squeezed her hand one last time and let it go. He tried to say something encouraging, but the words died on the tip of his tongue as her face fell.

"Mandy?" He cupped her ear, combing her curls out of the way. "What is it?"

Her gaze followed her hand, which dropped from his heart to his waist and slipped around to his back. "Please. Hold me. Just for a minu-ute."

The catch in her voice was his undoing, and he could do nothing but what she asked. It took only a half step to close the distance between them as he swallowed her in his embrace, one arm circling her waist and the other cradling her shoulders. He rocked back and forth, whispering nonsense words of love into her hair as a warm pool of tears seeped onto his shirt.

"Shh. It's all right now. You're safe."

"But I saw her."

"I know. She's gone now, though."

She hiccuped and leaned back just far enough to look into his eyes. "Before, I could lie to myself. I could pretend maybe, just maybe, she wasn't really after me."

"And now you can't."

She nodded, tucking back under his chin. "It's stupid, I know."

"It's not stupid. It's honest."

Her fingers brushed up and down his side. "Why are you so good to me?"

"Because we're in this together. Remember?" That got the little chuckle he'd been looking for. "Ready?"

"Almost." Pulling herself up on his shoulders, she pressed her lips to his.

Surprise made him tense for a split second, and she leaned back as if maybe the kiss had surprised her, too. Meeting her gaze, he shrugged and wrapped her in his arms again. Stumbling toward the tree trunk, he let her lean against the bark as he cupped her face with his hands.

She sighed as if he was the only thing she needed. Or would ever need.

"Kiss me?" she whispered.

One last tear on her cheek reflected the moonlight, and he swiped it away with this thumb.

Her lips were smooth and tasted of the strawberry-jelly sandwiches they'd snacked on earlier. His breath caught, everything vanishing. Everything except Mandy.

Her scent surrounded him, filling him with joy and wonder.

This.

This was all he'd ever wanted.

Even if he'd never met her, he'd have missed this.

He just wanted to hold her. Forever.

There went that line again.

God forgive him if this was wrong. But he wanted to love and honor this woman for the rest of his life, give her all that he had.

Even if all he had to give was his heart.

FOURTEEN

The next morning Mandy paced the kitchen for almost an hour before Luke clattered in on his crutches. His curls were adorably disheveled, and the early light glinted off his barely there stubble.

"Mom said you've been wearing a hole in the floor. Everything okay?"

She spun toward him, looking ready to unload all her worries but stopped short. "Did you injure your knee again? I told you, you have to be so careful. I'll take you to the hospital."

He held up his hand and shook his head as she tried to march by him. "I didn't injure it. It's just sore." She glanced up, trying to meet his eyes but having to settle for his jaw. "I figured my PT would appreciate it if I took it easy today. You know, rested it."

Ugh.

How did he do that? Every time she was ready to scold him for doing something extremely stupid in the name of saving her, he made her laugh instead.

It was starting to get annoying—mostly in the way that it was anything but annoying.

"It's probably wise, but you should still do your exercises today." She cringed at the way her voice wobbled. She pressed a hand to her stomach, which did a strange little dance any time he was this close. There was nothing to be done about the unique rhythm of her heartbeat.

Especially when she thought about that kiss the night before.

She jabbed both hands through her hair before covering her eyes. That had been such a terrible mistake. The worst.

Of course, if he hadn't propped her against the tree, she would have been a puddle at his feet. She'd wanted—needed—his comfort so badly. But still, she'd broken every one of her rules.

She was the one setting the boundaries, and she was the one crossing them, too. That had to stop. Any more of this, and her heart would truly be at risk.

It already was, if she was honest with herself.

But that couldn't possibly be God's plan. To lose her heart to another patient was ludicrous. She'd learned her lesson with Gary. If nothing else, God had used Gary to teach her that patients were off-limits.

Even someone who kissed her as if he could love her forever.

She scrubbed her fingertips across her scalp, wishing she could erase the memory and her embarrassment with it.

Luke obviously harbored no similar sentiments, if his Cheshire grin was any indication. "I thought you could help me with my exercises today."

"I have to go to the office."

Confusion crossed his features as his gaze swept over her work uniform. "Are you sure that's a good idea?"

"What am I going to do? Hide until she shows up here with a gun?" The words were hard to say but no less true. "I have patients to see and commitments to fulfill. I already took yesterday off. Besides, I won't be alone. The office is full of patients, and Tara is practically a guard dog."

He played with the corner of his mouth as his eyebrows

pulled together. "I can go to the office with you. I'll just do my session there."

She shook her head, reaching out to pat his arm, then yanking it back before making actual contact. Touching him wasn't going to help her say what she needed to.

"I think it's better if we…" She sighed and stared at the ceiling, praying for the right words. "Last night—there were so many emotions. I was terrified."

His eyes flashed with something close to anger, but it seemed mixed with agony. He leaned forward on his crutches, invading her personal space, almost daring her to back away. More likely daring her to keep going.

"We shouldn't have— I shouldn't have—kissed you. These feelings we have, they're an illusion."

His eyebrows rose until they disappeared under the swath of hair across his forehead. "Oh, really?"

She spun away, turned back and crossed her arms. Anything between them was better than nothing. "I'm sorry about last night. I shouldn't have instigated that…" Her hand fluttered near her forehead, her tongue unable to speak the word.

"Kiss." He didn't flinch. "I believe the word you're looking for is *kiss*. And it was pretty amazing from my point of view."

"Yes, well, of course. It was—you know—it was good." His eyebrow arched, a disbelieving scowl settling into place. "Fine. It was better than good. But it still shouldn't have happened. This thing between us is just a facade. It's the closeness between a PT and patient. It's the danger and fear and emotions that are just too much to handle. We have to stop all of it. Th-this—" She choked on the word, her heart catching up with her mouth and testifying against the lies she was telling.

But they had to be said.

No matter how much they hurt, she had to protect him

from the train wreck that their relationship would inevitably become if left unchecked.

"—isn't real."

His nostrils flared, his eyes narrowing as he cracked his neck.

But before he could speak, his phone went crazy, buzzing and squawking from deep in his pocket. He held up a finger to indicate that he wasn't finished with their conversation as he fished it out.

He glanced at the screen, then squinted back up at her. "Tristan says that symbol on the headstones is the Chinese symbol for revenge or payback."

Her stomach lurched, and she hugged her middle to keep from flying apart.

It was exactly what they had suspected. Someone wanted retribution for Laney's death and those of her parents.

"But he says this particular symbol is used almost exclusively for tattoos."

"How can he be sure?"

Luke read directly from the screen in his hand. "This symbol is a kind of slang that is generally only used by Chinese Americans and isn't very common outside the States or with classic Chinese speakers. It's a safe guess that whoever used this picked it up from a nonnative speaker. Most likely a tattoo artist."

"You think she has a revenge tattoo?" How much hate did it take to get a permanent reminder like that? Mandy squirmed at the very idea.

"Maybe."

"But she could be anyone."

He stared hard at his phone as if there might be more information on it. But when he looked up, he had only logic on his side. "Well, we know she's in Southern California—and probably has been since your identity-theft issues began. Tristan seems convinced she would have found that symbol at a tattoo artist's, so I think we should start asking around at local parlors. Maybe we'll catch a break."

It made sense. And she prayed they'd find something. Because they might not be able to dodge the next bullets.

Luke could barely think through the message from Tristan after the bomb Mandy had dropped. Since last night, he'd been completely sure of one thing. What was between them was absolutely real. He'd never loved anyone the way that he loved Mandy Berg.

And there was no doubt that she felt the same about him.

He just had to figure out how to get her to admit it.

But Tristan's message came first. Before he could tackle the problem of convincing Mandy that he was worth the risk, they had to figure out if Camilla—or anyone else— had gotten a revenge tattoo.

Swallowing the words that desperately wanted to be released, the words that might change her heart, he squeezed his phone until the urge passed. "I have a few connections with some tattoo shops in the area."

Her forehead wrinkled, and she crossed her arms. "You do?"

He shrugged. "A lot of navy men get ink."

"Including you?" It wasn't so much a question, but he felt compelled to correct her assumption.

"Actually, no. But I have some connections. I'll make some calls and stop by a few places today while you're in the office—but only if you promise me that you won't leave under any circumstances."

Arms still crossed and lips pinched, she nodded. "All right."

"And I'll follow you there."

She tossed up her hands. "You don't have to do that."

He didn't bother with a response to that. "I'll be ready to go in three minutes." He met her at the front door, ready to go, in two, and she didn't argue when he climbed into his car to follow her rental to the office. And while he never took his gaze off her taillights, his mind was sixty miles away. At the cemetery.

There had to be something about the Tracts that they had missed, something about Laney's sister, who had vanished. If she wasn't the one who had carved the revenge symbol on the headstones, she almost certainly would know who did.

Mandy pulled into her parking space at the side of the building and waved at him as she walked toward the glass doors. Luke started to wave back but jumped out to follow her inside. Catching her before she disappeared down the back hallway, he snagged her elbow, gave it a gentle tug and spun her around.

"Have you called Detective Fletcher about Laney's sister?"

"Not yet. I was going to do it today."

His gut said they couldn't wait. The same way he'd known that the suicide bomber in Lybania was trouble, he knew that Laney's sister was close. They couldn't risk another run-in like the night before. They most certainly couldn't count on a groundskeeper to unknowingly come to their rescue.

They had to put an end to this. Immediately.

A footstep in the hall drew his attention, and his gaze flicked over to the redhead toting her beach bag. "Tara." He nodded.

"Luke." Her tone was slightly surprised. "I don't think I have you on the schedule today. Should I put you in a slot?"

"He's not staying. He has to run some errands." Mandy squeezed his arm.

"Okay. But make that call about Laney's sister, all right?"

She nodded, shot Tara a smile and marched toward her office.

With furrowed brows, Tara leaned out over the front counter. "She okay? Any updates? Have they found Camilla yet?"

"Not yet. But I think we might be getting close. Do me a favor?"

"Anything."

"Keep an eye on Mandy today?" He stared down the hallway, then into Tara's bright blue eyes. "Don't let her leave until I'm back."

"Sure. Okay."

"What time's her last appointment today?"

She glanced down at her computer screen. "Five thirty."

"Great." With a pop of his fist on the counter, he walked out, got into his car and tried to figure out where to start with the hundreds of tattoo shops in the city.

After six hours and more than a dozen stops, Luke was beat and right where he'd started. He swiped the back of his hand over his forehead as he pulled into another gravel parking lot, another off-the-beaten-path house. The clock glared at him. Only three thirty. He had time for this and maybe one more place before he had to be at Mandy's.

He took his time crossing to the front entrance, every step another test on his knee. So far it was passing with flying colors.

As he swung open the door, a wave of smoke assaulted him, and he blinked away the tears that pricked his eyes. It was dark inside, and he wondered how any artist could work in these conditions. Still, he pushed toward a woman with a long black braid slung over her shoulder. Glancing up from the computer in front of her, she smiled.

"What can I do for you? Need some new ink?"

"I'm actually looking for someone who might have a specific tattoo."

Her smile dimmed. "Did they get it here?"

He shrugged, turning up the wattage on his smile until hers matched. "Maybe."

"Why do you need to find this person?"

"She's been harassing my..." How could he describe Mandy? *Physical therapist* was a little formal. *Friend* didn't come close to covering what he felt for her. "My girl."

"Show me the tattoo." He obliged, and her nose wrinkled. "Jimmy does most of our Chinese symbols. Let me ask him." She hollered loud and long until a short black man appeared from behind a gray curtain. "Hey, Jimmy, you give a tattoo like this recently?"

He looked at Luke's phone and plucked at the tip of his nose. "Revenge, huh? Well... I haven't done one of those in a while."

"On a woman?"

Jimmy perked up. "Only done two on women." As if the little man could read Luke's questions on his face, Jimmy answered them. "I remember every tattoo I've ever given, kind of like Picasso remembered every crazy painting he ever made. And that's just not a popular one for girls. Mostly it's angry boys with beady eyes asking for that."

Luke squeezed his fist at his side as his pulse picked up its pace. "Can you tell me anything about either of the women?"

"I can do you one better. I've got a picture."

"Seriously?"

Jimmy chuckled and ducked behind the curtain, re-appearing a moment later with a giant photo album that he plopped onto the counter. Flipping pages, he mumbled, "I like to keep visual records." They sailed past dragons and crosses, hearts and moons. Then Jimmy stopped and jabbed a finger at a picture.

The familiar symbol tattooed on a pale white, upper arm was clearly the object of the picture. Out of focus, a woman's profile looked down at her new ink, her flaming-orange hair tucked behind her ear.

Luke jerked away, his head snapping up and stomach taking a severe nosedive. "You're sure?" But it was a stupid question. Pictures didn't lie.

In fact this one had uncovered the biggest lie he'd ever known.

Racing out the door, he jabbed the button to call Mandy. *God, please let her answer. Please let her answer.*

Her phone went immediately to voice mail, and he slammed a fist against his steering wheel.

Scrubbing a hand down his face, he whispered, "God, just let me find her before it's too late."

Mandy waved to the young woman cradling her arm in a sling as she pushed open the front door. The teenager lifted one finger but didn't seem able to do much more.

Plopping the file down on the front desk, Mandy leaned an elbow on Tara's clipboard. "Is that the last one?" She hoped the empty waiting room wasn't a joke.

Tara offered a sympathetic smile. "That's it for the day. Your four thirty was the last."

Letting out a sigh, she glanced at her watch. "Is Luke back yet?" Tara shook her head, so Mandy nodded toward her office. "I'm going to make a quick phone call. Send Luke back if he gets here before I'm done."

If she hurried, she could call Detective Fletcher again. She'd had to settle for leaving a message earlier in the day, but she needed to know that he'd begun looking into the Tract family. Dialing the familiar number, she waited for him to answer and drummed her fingers against her desk. She almost hung up on the fifth ring, but it was snatched up just before the sixth.

"This is Ray Fletcher."

"It's Mandy Berg."

"I was just going to call you." His voice held a note of happiness, and his words tumbled out faster than she'd ever heard him speak before. "I'm on my way to the interview room right now. Camilla Heusen was picked up at the airport today on a return flight from Brazil."

"She's been in Brazil? But my office manager said she saw her…"

"Maybe just someone who looked like her. Mrs. Heusen has definitely been in Brazil for two weeks. Her passport stamps prove it."

Mandy's mind sped back over all of Gary's stories, trying to decipher the lies from the truth. "Can you tell me, is she wearing a wedding ring?"

"She is."

That jerk. Gary had lied about the whole thing. He'd lied about his divorce. He'd lied about being free to pursue her. Again. He'd lied about Camilla still being furious.

"Thank you. I think after you ask her a few questions, you'll find that she's completely ignorant of anyone stalking me."

He let out a low whistle. "You don't say."

"I'm pretty sure her husband set her up so that I'd feel sorry for him." She had a sudden urge to spit, her blood running so hot her head was nearly ready to fly off. "I think the woman after me is Laney Tract's sister. Can you look into her for me, see if you can locate her?"

"And why is she after you?"

Mandy propped an elbow on the desk and rested her face in her hand, the words making her entire heart twist. "I think she blames me for her family's deaths."

"I'm on it. I'll be back in touch. Stay close to that SEAL of yours until you hear from me."

She had to fight a smile as she hung up. Deep down, she liked the idea of Luke being *her* SEAL. Even if she'd told him just that morning that the kiss—kisses—had been a mistake. What her head knew to be true was a far cry from what her heart wanted.

And when she reached for her phone to find three missed calls from the object of far too many of her thoughts, she rubbed the back of her neck and hung her head. No call should elicit a flutter in her stomach like just seeing his name on her screen did.

"Hey, boss!" Tara called down the hall. "My car won't start, and I have to get to an appointment. Could you give me a jump?"

She glanced toward the hall, then back at the phone. She'd call him back as soon as she helped Tara.

Beach bag squarely on her shoulder, her manager stood by the back door, hands lifted in a what-are-you-going-to-do stance and a half smile in place. "Sorry about this."

"It's no problem," she said as they stepped outside.

Mandy slipped between their cars and opened her door to pop the hood. "Do you have jumper—" She turned to glance at Tara.

And she fell to the ground.

She'd been struck by lightning. It had to have been that. Everything inside her was on fire, explosions on every nerve. She curled into a ball, twitching hands covering the side of her neck, which somehow hurt worse than the rest of her. But how was that possible when she was already at a twelve from head to toe?

She tried to cry out for Tara's help, but her voice and all of her breath were gone.

A shadow stepped in front of the low-hanging sun, and she squinted at it, reaching for help.

Then the figure squatted in front of her. Blinking hard, she managed to bring Tara's face into focus. "Help. Me." The words didn't even make it past the ringing in her own ears.

"You have no idea how long I've been waiting to do that."

Mandy twitched, trying to pull away, but she seemed to have lost all of her faculties.

"Don't be afraid, Dr. Berg." Tara patted her head, and fireworks exploded behind her eyelids. "You're only getting what you deserve."

No. No. No. This couldn't be happening. It wasn't right. It couldn't be Tara. She was a coworker. A friend, even.

"Why?"

"Oh, we'll get to that soon enough. But first." She waved a Taser in her left hand before pressing it against bare skin.

Mandy's entire world exploded.

FIFTEEN

After the third call to Mandy with no answer, Luke chucked his phone across the car and slammed his fist against the steering wheel, hitting yet another red light. He revved the engine as sweat poured down his neck.

He had to get to her. He had to find her before Tara made her last move.

How had he missed it? How had he not seen the bitterness simmering below the surface? Or the rage in her eyes? She'd lost all connection with truth and blamed Mandy for the loss of her family and the pain that had followed. Tara had targeted one woman because she couldn't face the true source of her anguish—she'd been driving the car in the accident that paralyzed Laney.

It had been there in Jimmy's picture of the revenge tattoo. So clear, so obvious.

Tara was an incredible actress. That was all there was to it. She'd put on a production better than anything he'd ever seen on a stage. And she'd been playing the role for well over two years. She knew her part inside and out, and she'd fooled them all.

He slammed on the brakes again, waiting for the light to change.

Suddenly his phone buzzed from the passenger seat. He scooped it up and glanced at the text from Mandy.

Going for a walk. See you tonight.

That wasn't what they'd talked about. It wasn't what they'd agreed. She'd said she'd wait at the office. That she'd be safe.

With Tara.

His stomach rolled. When he covered his face, his hands shook like they never had in Lybania. And as he tried to take a breath, he choked on a sob he hadn't even known was there.

This wasn't like him. It wasn't normal.

Then again, this mission was as far from normal as he could get. Always in the field he could focus on getting the job done. He followed his training, watched his brothers' backs and finished strong.

But he'd never before been in love with the hostage. He'd never had to imagine the rest of his life without the most important person in it. Like a desert with no oasis, he already felt dry, sucked clean of the refreshing joy Mandy supplied.

"God, how can this be your plan? Any of this." He flung an arm around the car, encompassing the whole messed-up situation. His knee. Mandy's troubles. Laney's death. Tara's break with reality.

"What's going on?" He stared at the cloudless blue sky, hoping for an answer, even a sign he'd been heard. When nothing happened, he hung his head, his tone softening. "She needs me, and I can't get to her. Please just let her be at the office when I get there. Don't let Tara have taken her. Keep her safe."

As the light changed and cars parted, he peeled off the line. Zipping between other vehicles, he sailed onto the freeway, ignoring posted speed limits and praying again and again. *Keep her safe. I need her in my life.*

As he swerved off the freeway, his insides pulled into a knot. There was no telling what he'd find at the office.

Flying into the parking lot, he sped past Mandy's rental car. Tara's red hatchback was nowhere to be seen.

He galloped up the front steps and swung the front door open, his heart thundering and blood roaring his ears. "Mandy! Mandy! Are you here?"

Nothing.

Either she'd been taken.

Or worse.

He pounded down the hallway, poking his head into every room and closet, slamming doors behind him until he was sure. The place was deserted.

And Mandy never would have willingly left it open and unattended.

His phone rang, and he snatched it out of his pocket. "This is Dunham."

"Ray Fletcher here. I'm trying to reach Mandy Berg. Have you seen her?"

"I'm at her office right now, and she's gone. Kidnapped, I think."

Fletcher sucked in a harsh breath and slammed something that sounded like a desk drawer. "Laney Tract's sister fell off the grid just over two years ago."

"Yes. And she popped back up as Mandy's office manager right around that same time."

"Office manager?" Fletcher smacked his keyboard as if it had personally offended him. "Tara Sumner?"

Luke stood in the middle of the waiting room, turning a slow circle and praying for some clue that would point him in the right direction. "That's her. I think she's taken Mandy."

"Where would they have gone?"

"I have no—" Luke bit off his words, his mind flying back.

He had been standing in this very room, leaning against the front desk and talking with Tara. He'd been looking for a way into Mandy's affection. Tara had asked about his favorite beach spot. The deserted one where he had trained. She'd said she was looking for the perfect spot.

To do what?

His gut squeezed, and he nearly spit on the floor. "I think she took Mandy to this beach. It's pretty far off the beaten path, and the nearest lifeguard tower is blocked by a jetty, and the rocks keep the surfers away." He gave Fletcher the same directions he'd given Tara, every word grapefruit bitter as he prayed both that he was right and that he was wrong.

Mandy had to be there. He didn't know where else to look for her.

And if she was there, he'd given Tara the perfect place to dispose of a body.

"I'm on my way with backup." Fletcher ended the call before Luke could respond, which was probably better. Because no one was going to talk him into staying away.

"Get out of the car." Tara's growl was right next to her ear, and Mandy jerked away from the hot breath on her neck. She tried to wiggle deeper into the backseat of the car, but her shoulders ached from being tied behind her back. And the rest of her still thrummed to the tune of fifty thousand volts.

Tara grabbed her arm and yanked her from the car and into a deserted gravel lot. The rocks skinned her knees as she fell forward. Unable to stop herself, she tumbled face-first. Strangely, she couldn't even feel the abrasions on her cheeks and nose. They weren't enough to register when all she could think about was getting free. She had to find a way to run.

"Lord, help me," she whispered.

"Oh, He's not going to help you. Not after what you did, all the lives you ruined."

"What I did?"

Tara wrestled her to her feet and pushed her toward the sandy expanse at her back. Her blue eyes were wild, filled with a hatred unlike anything Mandy had ever seen. She snarled and snapped, a rabid dog finally released from its cage.

"Four years ago you refused to help my sister."

Mandy's foot slipped in the sand, and she went down on her knee. With a kick to her shoulder, Tara sent her all the way down. Spitting out sand, she tried to cry out, but only received another foot to her stomach for her trouble.

"Almost two years I've had to watch you pretend to be compassionate. Two years of you putting on this facade of kindness. You act like you really care about people, but when someone in real need comes to you, you toss her away like she's nothing. Nothing."

"Laney."

Tara flew at her, pinching her chin painfully between her thumb and forefinger. "No. You don't get to say her name. You don't even get to think about her."

Wrestling her way to her knees, Mandy nodded. There would be no negotiating or logical discussion. Right now Tara could see only the pain of loss, but maybe if Mandy kept her talking, she could survive until Luke found her.

Oh, Lord, how is he ever going to find me here?

She didn't even know where *here* was.

"What happened? After I saw La—" Mandy quickly changed direction at the fire in Tara's glare. "What happened to your family?"

"You know what happened to Laney."

She did. The poor girl had been heartbroken and chosen a bottle of pills over life in a wheelchair. "And your dad?"

"He started drinking—hard—after Laney died. Guess his liver couldn't take it."

"I'm sorry."

Getting right into her face, Tara swore vividly. "You think that apologizing is going to make up for my little sister or my dad? You think it'll make up for my mom, who just couldn't live without them? She gave up after dad died. Quit sleeping and eating. I moved her to San Diego with me, but she was already half-gone. And do you know who found her in her bed that morning? She was so cold and her skin was white."

"Oh, Tara."

"If you had only given Laney a chance. If you'd just *tried* to help her…" Tara's mouth pinched with hatred, and she spat the words like venom. "If you had done your job, none of this would have happened. I'd still have my family. All of them."

Tears rushed to Mandy's eyes, and with her hands pinned, she let them flow uninhibited.

"Oh, what? Now *you* want *me* to feel sorry for you?"

"No. I'm just so sorry about what happened to your family." Her lip quivered and she bit into it, tasting the sand and seawater.

Tara hitched her arm through Mandy's and dragged her back on her heels. "You took everything from me, so I set out to do the same to you."

Suddenly all the pieces of the puzzle fit. Tara, who had sorted her office mail and had access to all of her personal information, had stolen her identity and tried to get her accreditation revoked. Tara had been making her life miserable, but why try to kill her now?

"And then you think you'll just run away to Miami and all your problems will stay here?"

The flowers. The job offer. She'd only halfway considered it, but she'd mentioned it to Tara. Right before the attempted hit-and-run.

All of this was because she couldn't help a young woman who wasn't stable enough to take on the pressures of physical therapy. And because she'd thought running away from her problems might have been easier than facing them.

Her stomach heaved. She was going to be sick.

"You still owe me for the pain you caused. When that stupid Gary showed back up, I knew it was time to make you pay. And when they find your body, they'll think it was an accidental drowning."

"But the stun-gun marks. There'll be an investigation, an autopsy."

Tara leaned in close, her breath hot and moist. "I'll be long gone by then."

Waves lapped at her feet, and Mandy wrenched herself free, scrambling for safety but falling in the shifting sand. In a split second Tara was on her, shoving her toward the water. "You deserve this. You should have helped my baby sister."

"There was nothing I could do."

"You could have fixed her!" Tara jabbed a finger into her chest, forcing her into knee-deep water. Cold waves crested and pushed against her, and she had to hold herself together, every muscle tight, just to stay standing. "I've seen you fix those ungrateful rich snobs. Why didn't you help Laney?"

A groan from deep within tore out of her, and Mandy doubled over at the pain in her heart, the aching in her chest. "I didn't want her to give up." She hadn't. At all. And she'd tried to get the girl help. It just hadn't been enough for a heart that had been more broken than her body. "I'm so sorry."

"It's too late now." With a snarl, Tara lunged, tackling her in the water and holding her under.

Mandy thrashed and kicked, squirming and fighting

for air. But with her hands tied and already depleted from Tara's abuse, she knew she couldn't keep it up for long. Her muscles grew numb from the cold, and her lungs screamed for oxygen. Just a breath. Anything but the endless expanse of the Pacific.

She swallowed a swimming pool's worth of water, gagging and choking in even more.

But she couldn't die yet.

Not while Luke thought she believed what she'd told him that morning.

She'd been trying to protect herself. To protect him. She'd been terrified of repeating the mistakes that she'd made with Gary. Afraid that she'd lose herself again.

Except Luke didn't make her disappear, he gently prodded out the very best, the bravest, the truest parts of her. She was the best version of herself with him because he asked nothing, but he'd given everything.

Why had she been so scared? Why hadn't she taken every single opportunity to hold him tightly and to tell him that she loved him?

And she did love him!

She wasn't afraid anymore. And now she had nothing to lose. She was dead anyway.

With a spin and a kick to Tara's stomach, she sailed through the water, surfacing a few yards away. The water tossed her about as she gulped the salty air and fought to find her footing. Splashing and writhing toward shore, her foot caught on a patch of slimy seaweed, slowing her down just enough for Tara to shove her below the surface and hold her there.

Luke spied Tara's car as soon as he rounded a bend in the road. He sent gravel flying as he skidded to a stop beside it. No sign of the cops yet. Slamming his car door, he scanned the horizon. There, on the other side of twenty yards of sand and silhouetted by the setting orange sun, two figures thrashed in the water.

Mandy didn't seem to be using her arms, but other than that, she was putting up a pretty good fight.

His foot slid in the dry sand, and he stopped with jarring speed. Mandy had warned him off unstable ground again and again. It wasn't safe. His knee could be twisted and the ligaments torn. And if he injured his knee a second time, his chances of returning to the teams would disappear.

Gazing from his knee brace to the sand to Mandy, he knew. There wasn't even a question in his mind.

He could figure out civilian life.

But he couldn't begin to imagine his life without Mandy.

Sprinting across the sand was both familiar and frightening. He'd run hundreds of miles on the Coronado Beach. His feet knew how to land, his muscles remembered how to move. But he couldn't help the voice in his mind reminding him that if he fell, he wouldn't reach her in time.

Mandy's form disappeared beneath the water, Tara hovering over her, a deranged smile splitting her face.

Lord, keep me on my feet.

It took hours to reach her. It took only seconds. Finally and suddenly, he made it, pushing Tara to the side and scooping Mandy's limp form from the sea.

Tara burst out of the water like a sea monster, her arms flailing and eyes wild as she clung to him. "She deserves this. She killed my sister!"

Luke flung her off his back, charging for solid ground. "I'm pretty sure you were driving the car."

Tara froze, her mouth hanging open and a hand on her cheek as though his words had been a physical slap. The approaching sirens seemed to jerk her from her stupor, and she took off at a slow run through the water.

He couldn't chase her just then. He had more important

things to worry about. Mandy's unresponsive body rested against his chest, her head lolled back, her chest unmoving.

She wasn't breathing.

Setting her on the sand, he knelt over her, using his pocket knife to cut the zip tie around her wrists before checking first for a breath—nothing—and then a pulse, thready but steady. Angling her neck, he plugged her nose and sealed his mouth over hers. He released a hard breath, and her chest rose. Then again. And again.

And then she coughed hard, half of the Pacific spewing from her mouth. He rolled her to her side, letting her empty her stomach. After several heaves, she fell back, eyes closed but chest definitely rising and falling in a regular rhythm.

Pressing his palm to her cheek, careful to avoid the red abrasion there, he leaned in. "Mandy? Can you hear me?"

She covered his hand with hers. "I'm here." The words were more croak than melody, but they still filled his chest, blooming like flowers in spring. The vise on his heart fell away, and it beat normally for the first time in hours.

"You had me worried there, Doc."

She patted his hand, her eyes still closed, a tiny smirk wiggling into place. "Took your sweet time getting here, didn't you?"

"Well, you didn't exactly leave me a map."

"Obviously I would have, if I hadn't been stunned."

His insides felt as if they'd been jabbed with a fork. "Oh, honey. I'm sorry." He brushed her sopping hair out of the way and ran a gentle thumb near the twin burns on her neck. She flinched and gasped. "I know. It hurts. But you're going to be okay. We'll get you some help."

Her lashes fluttered open, her eyes filled with equal parts pain and relief. "You been stunned before?"

Memories of being thrown into the deep end of a pool, hands and feet tied, during SEAL training brought an em-pathetic smile. "And drowned, too. You're going to be fine."

Slipping her fingers between his, she gave his hand a slow squeeze. "'Cause we're in this together. 'Member?"

"Yes. I remember."

Except there was no more *this*.

Two policemen were dragging a waterlogged Tara across the beach, her head hung low, her fight gone. The operation was complete. Mandy had nothing left to fear. She had no more need of his protection.

But losing her wasn't an option. And if it had to become his lifelong mission, he would show her they were better together.

SIXTEEN

"Where do you think you're going?"

Mandy snapped up from tying her shoes to find Ashley Waterstone standing at her screened back door, one hand on her hip, the other cradling a brown paper bag of groceries.

She hopped up and ran across her small kitchen to let her in. "What are you doing here?"

"Well, I thought I was coming to check on the invalid." Ashley's blond ponytail bounced with her teasing.

Mandy laughed, the sound rich and true, bouncing off the white cupboards. "Staci and Jess were just here yesterday. I'm fine." When Ashley arched an eyebrow, Mandy rushed to reassure her. "Re-eally." Oh, dear. That hitch in her voice was a dead giveaway, and her friend latched on to it like a fisherman reeling in his catch.

Setting the bag on the counter, Ashley crossed her arms and leaned a hip against the counter. "We've known each other since Matt's rehab, so there's no need to pretend with me. You've been through something awful, and no one would fault you for needing a little bit of time. It's only been four days."

Mandy stared at her empty hands, suddenly needing something to do. "Let me make you some coffee." She opened the wrong cabinet and laughed at herself. "I guess

I'm still getting used to being in my own home." It felt as if she'd been displaced for years instead of a few days. But so much had happened in that short amount of time.

"Honey, do you want to talk about it?"

No. She had no desire to talk about Tara or her trip to the police station to make a statement against the madwoman. She didn't want to rehash the pain of being attacked yet again or the fear she'd felt in the moment before she passed out underwater. Or the sheer joy of hearing Luke's deep voice when she woke up.

She'd already spent enough sleepless nights reliving, rebreathing those moments.

What she really wanted was to know why Luke hadn't called her since the beach.

The sick feeling deep inside was all the explanation she needed. After all, she'd told him what they'd shared wasn't real and they couldn't be together. She'd pushed him away after their life-altering kiss.

But most of all, she wanted to know how any of this could be part of God's plan.

The pain, the struggles and turmoil—those were for her growth, right? Scripture said something about rejoicing in suffering because it developed character. It wasn't fun. It wasn't easy, but she was growing, becoming more the woman she wanted to be and less the selfish, blind one.

Those hurts weren't wasted.

But the broken heart?

She wasn't sure what that was for.

Ashley reached for the mug she offered, and Mandy poured another for herself. Pressing the cup to her lips and inhaling the sharp steam of the dark roast, she closed her eyes and tried to think about anything except Luke. It wasn't easy when his face had been tattooed on her mind's eye.

"It's just that he hasn't called." Could she possibly sound any more pathetic?

Ashley offered a gentle smile of encouragement, and suddenly the words were pouring out of her mouth as if Mandy had no filter. "I told him early on that we couldn't be more than patient and therapist, but he just climbed over that wall like it was a footstool. And then I told him the worst—the absolute worst thing I've ever done—and he didn't even flinch. It was like he saw the best in me and refused to believe I was the same woman."

"You're not, you know."

Mandy's gaze swung from her coffee to Ashley's face.

"I didn't know you very well back then, and what I did know, I liked a lot. You were a great physical therapist and a kind woman. But after Gary, you had this compassion that I hadn't seen before. The way you talked with the women at PCH, it was clear you knew what it was like to be emotionally battered. And Luke might have mentioned to Matt how impressed he was when you told Gary to get lost or you'd slap a restraining order on him."

She threw a hand over her eyes. "He didn't."

"Oh, he definitely did. And the old Mandy never would have stood up for herself like that." Ashley squeezed her hand, furrowed her brows and leaned in close. "You don't have to be afraid of making the same mistakes that you made before, because God is changing you.

"And you're in a doubly good place because Luke is the kind of guy who will bring out the very best in you."

A tear slid down Mandy's cheek, and she knuckled it away. If that was really true, then she was suffering this broken heart for no good reason.

Suddenly her phone vibrated, and she jumped to pick it up off the table. Luke.

Her mouth went dry as she flashed the screen at Ashley.

"Answer it," she whispered.

Mandy cleared her throat and did her best to sound put together when she said, "Hey, Luke."

"Hi." He paused, and the silence was filled only with the deafening thump of her heart. "So, I think there might be something going on with my knee."

She flipped the switch to professional mode in an instant. "You have to get it checked out. If you can't get an appointment with your orthopedist today, go to the ER."

"I was actually wondering if you would take a look at it."

"Me?" The word squeaked out, and Ashley shot her a smile.

"Could you meet me at your office in an hour?"

"All right."

Luke took a giant breath and let it out slowly. Then he pulled on the handle of the glass door. The blinds rattled at about the same tempo as his heart, and he scrubbed a hand down his face.

He hadn't been this nervous when he'd started BUD/S.

But he'd given her four days of space, and he couldn't wait another.

"Mandy?" he called into the empty office.

"I'm in the back room."

When he reached her, she was busy wiping down the exercise equipment. "Hop up on the table." She flashed him a smile over her shoulder, but if he wasn't mistaken, it carried a definite note of uncertainty.

Then he would just have to be certain enough for the both of them.

Sitting on the table, he swung up his leg and undid his brace. The Velcro cried as it released, especially loud in the otherwise empty building.

Her head still bent over a large exercise ball, she said, "I told you not to walk on sand. Why'd you do it?"

"I just did what anyone else would have done."

"Really?" She shook her head, stood, wiped her hands down her pants and ran her fingers through her hair. It hung loose and long, a change from the ponytail she usually wore at work, and he had to fist his hands at his hips to keep from reaching for her.

"Because I think anyone who wanted back on the teams wouldn't have been so careless."

He tipped his chin down, raising his eyebrows. "Seriously. You're going to get on my case for saving your life?"

She squirted a glob of hand sanitizer in her palm and rubbed it in. "You're right. I should probably just say thank you." She gave him another off-kilter smile.

"You don't have to—"

She cut him off quickly, clearly needing to change the subject. "So how's it feeling? Where does it hurt?"

Okay, so it was going to be like that. Professional mode. He could play that game.

"Pretty good."

She wrapped her hands around his calf and gave it a gentle tug, bending and stretching the joint. Glancing up, she watched his face, but he couldn't stop the smile there.

"There isn't any swelling or redness. Is it tender when I pull on it?"

He shook his head. "Not really."

"Does it hurt when you walk on it?"

"No."

Her lips twisted into a strange frown. "Then what makes you think there's a problem? It looks good to me. We can go in for an MRI, but honestly, I think you're okay. There's no new damage. And if you don't make it a habit of running on the beach for a while, then you're probably okay."

"I know."

Her gaze snapped to his, her eyebrows pinched together and the tip of her nose wrinkled. "Then why did you call?"

"I needed an excuse to see you, so I might have stretched the truth a little bit."

"A little?"

He shrugged, swung his legs off the table and pulled her in front of him. "I'm a little sore, but it's from using muscles that I haven't gotten to use in a while."

She folded her hands in front of her, staring at her fingers for a long moment. "Then why...?"

Finally he released himself to touch a loose wave of hair flowing over her shoulder. It was like fine silk and ten times prettier, and it smelled like the beach at sunrise.

"Because I think what you said the other morning is right. The stress we've been under, tension and fear, elevates emotions."

"Oh." Her shoulders fell, and she wrapped her arms around her middle, taking two quick steps back. He'd just bungled that.

Fix it, Dunham.

He scrambled for the right words. "But that doesn't make what I feel for you any less real." The corner of her mouth quirked. It wasn't a smile, but it was close. So he kept going. "When I met you, I thought life as I knew it was over. Everyone else told me I wasn't ever going to make it back on the teams. You told me to put in the effort. My ex-girlfriend said I wasn't a good gamble. You saw something worth your time." Walking his fingers around her waist, he gave her a little tug and closed half the gap between them.

"I couldn't see how any of this could be part of God's plan. How could this injury ever be a good thing? And then I met you. You gave me a mission and a purpose and reminded me that I have something to give the world, even if I can't ever return to the teams. And I saw that everything I'd been through had brought me right to you—from my injury to picking locks. God used all of it to bring us together. So when I got to that beach the other night, I didn't even have to question going after you. If I had lost you, I'd have lost my heart."

She bit her lips until they disappeared, her eyes glistening. But she didn't say anything. The emotional silence sent his veins thrumming and his eyes burning. Why didn't she say something?

The silence was too much. "I know you said that there couldn't be an *us* as long as I'm your patient, so if you want me to find another physical therapist, I will. If you want to wait until I'm done working with you, I will. If you just need some time to think about things, I'll give you time.

"But I just need you to know that I'm completely in love with you."

She laughed out loud at that, a sharp hiccup of surprise. The corners of her eyes crinkled, and she pressed her hand over his good knee.

"I mean, whatever you—"

She pressed her fingers to his lips as a very slow smile worked its way across her mouth. "I was afraid. I was afraid of making the same mistakes with you that I'd made before. I tried so hard to push you away. Maybe because I knew you were special. But I don't want to do that anymore."

His sudden grin was so wide it hurt. Plunging his fingers into her hair, he leaned his forehead against hers. "So that means…"

"We're in this together."

He crushed his lips against hers, unable to wait even a second longer. In his arms she was a summer rainstorm over the ocean, refreshing and all consuming. Her scent surrounded him, her heartbeat setting a breakneck pace for his own. As she ran her fingers along his jaw, he pulled back, the fog around his brain parting.

In that moment of clarity, his mouth dropped open. "I just told you that I love you."

She rested her hands on his chest and shot him a lop-sided grin. "Mmm-hmm."

"And you didn't say it back."

"Didn't I?" She pressed her nose into his neck. His stomach pitched like a barrel on the open sea. And he wondered if he'd ever get used to holding her in his arms.

He cleared his throat. "I don't think— No. No, you didn't."

"Then I suppose I better remedy that." And she did.

EPILOGUE

Seven months later

The blinds on the front door smacked together as it slammed shut, and Barb, Mandy's new office manager, yelled, "This is a place of healing. Not a playground."

The pounding footsteps stopped immediately, and Luke said, "Yes, ma'am."

Mandy laughed from her chair behind her own desk, imagining Barb glaring over her reading glasses at the young man she secretly adored. She'd never admit it, but when he wasn't there, Barb couldn't stop talking about what a kind, courteous, handsome young man he was.

Mandy tended to agree, but she was probably biased.

"She's in her office," Barb said.

The footsteps got louder, and her stomach filled with a thousand butterflies. Even still, he had the power to make her smile on the spot.

"Getting in trouble again, Dunham? Have you learned nothing?"

His laugh made the butterflies take flight as he rounded the corner, waving a bouquet of yellow roses just below his chin.

"Oooh. For me?" She jumped out of her chair and ran around the edge of her desk. "What's the occasion?"

He shrugged a shoulder. "Oh, nothing big. I just got cleared for active duty today."

She squealed and jumped into his arms, hugging his neck with all her might. He tightened an arm around her waist, lifted her up and spun in a quick circle. She laughed right in his ear, running her hands over his freshly cut curls.

As he set her back on her feet, she whispered, "I am so proud of you."

His smile wouldn't quit as he pulled her palm to his lips, kissing the very center of it. "I couldn't have done it without you."

"Oh, I know." She held back her giggle for as long as she could until her face broke, and it came tumbling out. "You worked so hard. And I love you so much."

And he had. It had taken weeks of therapy and months of training to get back into shape, but he'd never complained. And he'd never quit.

She dropped her flowers into the vase that he kept full—always with yellow roses. He'd announced they were their thing and had promptly set about making them her new favorite.

"So, are we going to the barbecue at Ashley and Matt's or what?" she asked.

Ashley, ever the hostess, had planned a party as soon as her brother Tristan had announced his retirement from active SEAL duty two weeks before. Luke, Will, Zach, Jordan and the rest of the team had ribbed Tristan for getting old, but as a husband and dad of four adopted kids, his priorities had shifted. "Besides, every time I deploy, Staci decides it's time to adopt another kid," he'd joked. Only it wasn't too far from the truth.

Now it was time to celebrate his new assignment, as a BUD/S instructor. Future SEAL classes were going to learn from the best.

But if they didn't hurry, they'd be late to the festivities. "Let me just grab my bag."

Luke stopped her with a hand on her wrist, giving it a gentle tug that spun her right back into his arms. She landed with a palm flat over his heart, and it was racing.

"Luke?" His smile wobbled, and he swallowed twice in a row. "What are you doing? We have to go."

"I know. And I was going to wait until…well, until a better time."

She could barely catch a breath. "For what?"

He licked his lips, and his Adam's apple bobbed again.

"Luke Dunham? What is going on? You're shaking."

"I know." He laughed. "I didn't think I'd be so nervous."

"Nervous? What on earth are you talking about?"

Suddenly he dropped to a knee, almost as if he was stretching his hip flexor. She'd seen him do that a hundred times. But this posture, this scenario was different.

With a gasp, she threw her hands over her mouth.

"I was going to do this right, with a big night on the town and a fancy dinner and a walk on the beach in the moonlight. And I'll do all those things for you. But I just can't wait to ask." He dug into his pocket and pulled out a small black velvet box.

"Doctor Mandy Berg, will you marry me?"

"Say yes!" Barb cried from down the hall.

They exploded with laughter, and she fell to her knees in front of him, draping her arms over his shoulders. With tears of joy streaming down her cheeks, she whispered against his mouth, "Petty Officer Luke Dunham, I'm all yours."

And he was all hers.

* * * * *

Dear Reader,

I'm beyond grateful that you've joined me and the men of SEAL team fifteen for another Men of Valor book. I hope you enjoyed Luke and Mandy's story as much I enjoyed writing it.

I first introduced Luke in *Navy SEAL Noel*, and I loved him from his first appearance on the page. I knew he needed a strong heroine by his side, and Mandy fit the bill. I love how these two bring out the very best in each other.

As Mandy struggles to forgive herself for her past mistakes, Luke tries to figure out what his future will look like. And I think we all grapple with both the past and what's to come. As you deal with those things in your own life, I hope that Mandy and Luke will remind you that God's plans are much greater than our own, and He makes beautiful things out of the messes we see.

Thanks for spending your time with us. I'd love to hear from you. You can reach me at liz@lizjohnsonbooks.com, Twitter.com/LizJohnsonBooks or Facebook.com/LizJohnsonBooks. Or visit LizJohnsonBooks.com to sign up for my newsletter.

Liz Johnson